Home Ice

by
USA Today bestselling author
Catherine Gayle

Dedication

For Heather, Kaelyn, Lexi, and Killian. And for Christi, Rory, Reagan, and Riley.

Acknowledgments

Thank you to my friend Christi Caldwell for pointing me in the right direction when it comes to all things related to raising a child with Down syndrome.

Chapter One

Paige

"OH MY GOD." My eldest daughter, Zoe, stopped dead in her tracks, her face completely pale as though she'd just seen a ghost.

Her sudden halt caused a pileup of my girls, all screeching to a standstill right beside her. The huge crowd surrounding us in the concourse at the Moda Center—all here for the Portland Storm's StormSkillz Competition, the same as we were—nearly ran our little group over in their quest to get food and drinks and get to their seats for the day of family fun.

Clueless as to what led my girls to cause a traffic jam, I took a cursory look around, but all I could see was the ocean of purple and silver jerseys jockeying for position. Nothing stood out as being anything that should cause that kind of reaction in my sixteen-year-old daughter. "What?" I asked, since I didn't have the first inkling what was going on.

Zoe looked like she might have stopped breathing.

Her younger sisters had figured it out, though. Evie, my fifteen-year-old, clutched her older sister's hand and let out a squeal, her face turning twenty-seven shades of pink and red with excitement. "It's Levi Babcock! Right there."

Well, that explained it. My girls were seriously boy crazy—all four of them—and Levi Babcock was their obsession du jour. Zoe was even wearing a Storm jersey that had "Future Mrs." as the name and 501 as the number. Apparently, everyone called him 501 because of his name and the jeans, or something like that. I had a hard time keeping up with all the preoccupations kids talked about these days. There was just too much on my plate.

I spun around, and that was when I found him—tall, broad, dark-haired, wearing a designer suit. A few other men in suits were around him, which made them stand out among the jersey-clad fans filling up the building. They were probably all players, or at least involved with the team in some way. Why else would they be in suits? My girls didn't have eyes for any of them but Levi, though. In recent years, I had come to learn that female teens had a certain type of hormone that produced single-minded determination in a way that I didn't quite recall experiencing. Surely I couldn't have been too different from my girls, though. Maybe I'd just blocked it all from memory due to embarrassment.

The young Storm defenseman should probably run away, and fast, because I didn't know if I would be able to control all four of my hormone-riddled daughters, and if they got their hands on him... I shook my head. I'd probably be doing good to keep any *one* of them in check, but all *four*? The end result could be disastrous for the young man.

Zoe's jaw was hanging open, her eyes popping out of her head in a way that was downright comical; Evie was practically hyperventilating, her skin flushed; Izzy, my thirteen-year-old, had started bouncing in circles and was talking in a nonstop stream of high-pitched babble that sounded like *oh-Mom-can-we-go-meet-him-and-get-his-autograph-and-kidnap-him-right-now-please-I-promise-I'll-take-good-care-of-him-he-can-be-my-first-brother-husband-then-we-just-have-to-kidnap-Kaner-and-Seguin-and-Torey-Krug-too.*

And then there was my youngest, eleven-year-old Sophie. As with everything in life, Sophie was a special case. She stopped alongside her sisters long enough for it to seep in that her crush was standing not twenty feet away from us, and then she was off like a shot.

"Shit," I muttered beneath my breath, taking off after her and calling out, "Sophie, stop right this second! Help me with your sister," I added over my shoulder to the other three, in the hope that they could pull themselves together enough to do what needed to be done.

I needed all hands on deck, because when Sophie had her mind set on something, it was next to impossible to veer her off her intended course. A mean stubborn streak went along with the territory with my youngest, as was common in kids who had Down syndrome. Not that she was mean; she was just obstinate about getting what she wanted. She was actually one of the sweetest, kindest, most loving and loveable kids I'd ever known, but at the moment, she wanted to give all of her love—whether it was welcome or not—to an unsuspecting Levi Babcock.

"Levi!" she shouted as she raced toward him, ducking between people traveling in every direction around her. She only had eyes for her prey, though, oblivious to everything else going on.

Levi swiveled his head around, trying to determine where the voice had come from, and caught sight of her just in time. He broke into an easy grin, but I doubted he understood that he was her intended target and was about to get pummeled with affection. Sophie launched herself at him, and he barely got his arms out and ready to catch her in time, his grin disappearing in exchange for wide-eyed surprise. Being smaller, stronger, and far more determined than I was, my little girl had made it through the crowd in a flash.

I pushed my way through the throng, desperate both to get to my daughter and to apologize for her overzealous behavior. A lot of people in this world just didn't understand, and some weren't very forgiving. I had no way of knowing which category Levi might fall into. Zoe, Evie, and Izzy were right on my tail, which was good, since I might need backup.

We arrived just in time to hear Sophie ask him, "Levi, will you marry me?"

A genuine smile lit up his features and brought out a dimple in his left cheek as he held my daughter high up in his arms. Hers were wrapped so tight around his neck that she had to be making breathing difficult, but he didn't seem to mind. No wonder my girls were all head over heels in puppy love with this guy. I probably would be, too, if I were their age.

He winked at Sophie, and then he nodded over at me. "I'm not so sure your mom is ready to give you up just yet," he said, deftly brushing off her proposal without doing so in a way that would hurt her feelings. "How about we see how things stand in a decade or so? You might meet someone you like better than me by then, you know. I might get old and fat and lose my hair."

"I'll never love anyone better than you." Sophie put her head down on his shoulder, her expression as blissful as I'd ever seen it.

"I'm sorry," I said, trying to pry her death grip free, but she was on him like duct tape with no intention of letting go. "Sophie, honey, we have to let Levi go get ready to skate."

"Actually, no, you don't," one of the other men in suits said. He had a deep, accented voice that rumbled through me, and I shot my gaze up to his, fully ready to give him a piece of my mind about telling my kid something that directly went against what I'd just told her. It was hard enough to get her to listen as it was, sometimes, and the last thing I needed was someone giving her the wrong impression.

Then I started suffering from a case of the same hormonal chaos that had taken over my daughters. I had no idea who this man was—huge, muscled, with a strong jaw and a full head of salt-and-pepper hair that was perfectly styled, not to mention blue-gray eyes that had no business being anywhere but the bedroom—but simply looking at him stole my ability to form a more coherent thought than *unh* at the same time as it made my knees suddenly go weak.

This was trouble. I had too much on my hands already to deal with jumping back in time to my own teen years.

Then he smiled at me, and I feared I might thoroughly disgrace myself in front of my girls and let rapid-onset jelly-legs syndrome take over my life. I hadn't gone gaga over a man in years, but apparently I wasn't immune to it.

"Mom, I *told* you I was gonna marry Levi," Sophie said, her smile bright enough to light up Times Square at New Year's.

That was all it took to remind me I was the grown-up here, and I had a job to do. Sophie still had a death grip on Levi's suit jacket, but he wasn't acting anxious to be rid of his ardent and very much too young so-called fiancée.

I steeled my spine for the task at hand—figuring out a way to extricate her without either ripping his jacket or instigating a temper tantrum—and reached for her again. "Maybe someday," I said, trying to pry her stubby fingers free. "But it's going to have to wait. He's got to do work today."

"That's what I was saying," the drop-dead gorgeous older man said.

He gently eased Sophie's grip open and lifted her out of Levi's arms, setting her down on the ground. More than that, she *let* him do that. Sophie didn't let anyone get away with something like that so easily. There was something about this man that made her trust him, and I wasn't sure if that was a good thing or a bad thing. My hormones were leaning toward the good thing part, but trusting *them* to make decisions for me wasn't something I could—or should—do.

"What were you saying?" I asked, mentally telling my hormones to get in line, or else. Ha. Like they'd ever paid attention to my threats.

"There's nothing he has to do today except cater to you and your girls," the older man said, grinning at Sophie.

That smile? The way he was looking at my baby girl? That was a panty-melting move for me, only I wasn't positive he meant it to be one.

I shook my head. "I'm sorry. My head's in the clouds and I'm not quite following."

"I'm not either," Levi said. "What am I supposedly doing today?"

My girls all tittered nervously, blushing up a storm, just because he'd opened his mouth. He could speak gibberish, and their response would be the same. Still, he was as lost as I was about this whole thing. At least I wasn't the only one confused.

That amazing smile turned to me. Cue panty explosion.

"Sorry. I'm Mattias Bergstrom, the Storm's head coach." He held out a hand, but I was too nervous to shake it.

"Paige Calhoun," I spluttered. "And my daughters, Zoe, Evie, Izzy, and Sophie."

Then he kept going, dropping his hand back to his side as though I hadn't just been exceedingly rude. "In our last game, 501 got tripped up and hit his head on the goal post. He had some concussion symptoms that night, so we've got to hold him out of all activity for at least a week. That means he can't take part in any of today's events…which means he gets to be your personal companion for the day. All day long, he's going to take care of you five ladies. He'll take you up to the press box to show you around. He'll sit with you through the different events and explain whatever you want him to explain. After it's over, he'll bring you back down to the locker room and introduce you to the boys so you can get autographs. He's going to make today special for you and your girls."

"He is?" I spluttered at the same time as Levi said, "I am?"

I shook my head. "There's got to be some sort of

mistake here, some confusion." I reached for Sophie's hand, determined to corral my girls and head toward our seats without any further boy issues. "We've just got regular tickets for the event. Nothing special. We should go." I tugged on Sophie's hand, but she didn't budge.

"Mom," she said in the long, drawn-out way that was unique to her when she was annoyed with me. "We're spending the day with *Levi*."

"There's no mistake," the coach said. "The other coaches and I will help him out where we can, but I want to make this happen." He looked off to the side at a gray-haired man with glasses, another one of the suits who'd been listening with a good deal of interest and a slight smile. "We can make this happen, can't we, Jim?"

"I don't see why not," the older man said. "Rach—"

"Not to worry. I'm already on it," a petite redheaded woman said, stepping into our circle. Even with only those few words, I could hear her thick Southern accent. She definitely wasn't originally from around here. She fished through a messenger bag for a moment and came up with a handful of passes on neck straps. She counted off five and handed them over to me. "Be sure you're wearing these at all times. Just keep them around your necks. They'll get you access to wherever Bergy wants 501 to take you." She smiled at me, then at each of my girls. "I think y'all are going to have a great day."

With fierce determination, Sophie released my hand, took her badge, settled it around her neck, and reached for Levi's hand. The whole time, she was grinning from ear to ear.

I supposed that settled that. With a sigh of resignation, I handed the other girls their badges and put one around my own neck. "I guess we're getting the royal treatment today, girls."

Not that I didn't want to give them the world. I did, and they knew I would do everything I could for them. I didn't make a ton of money as a massage therapist, though, and I worked hard for every penny I earned. Their father paid child support, but that money only went so far. The only reason we were here at all today was because he had won tickets in a raffle at work, but he had to be out of town this weekend. He couldn't bring the girls. That left it to me to corral them and herd them in the direction of our destination without veering off our course too far, as usual, and so here we were.

Coach Bergstrom winked at Sophie, and my knees almost gave out on me. There was apparently something about a man looking after my little girl like this that did me in.

"Let me have a word with 501, ladies, and then I'll leave you in his hands."

I JERKED MY head to the side for Levi Babcock to follow me a few steps away from Paige Calhoun and her daughters. He came, but not without a stowaway attached to him at the hip. Sophie, the little girl who reminded me so much of my sister, wouldn't release his hand, leaving my young defenseman with a comically bewildered and anxious expression. Not that I could blame him for his nerves.

Much like most hockey players, Levi was better

known by his nickname, 501, than by his given name. He was a lot like his older brother, Jamie, a guy everyone called Babs. They both had the sort of youthful good looks that brought out screaming teenaged girls in droves, like they were in a boy band or something. Babs was engaged to be married now, so he could always use his fiancée as an excuse to get away from his more overzealous admirers, but 501 didn't have the same luxury. He was fair game, as far as they were concerned.

That meant he had to be careful. I understood that even if I'd never experienced anything like it myself. Some of those girls might try to trap him, and then he'd have a world of problems to sort out, both personal and potentially legal. Not something he needed to add to his plate right now. Our general manager, Jim Sutter, and I had already given him plenty to work on as soon as he was medically cleared to return to the ice. He didn't need to add any off-ice issues to his agenda right now.

This girl was not one he needed to be wary of, though, and I didn't need to know her personally in order to be certain of that fact.

I smiled at Sophie. She gripped 501's hand harder and hugged her cheek to his arm, oblivious to the look of panic in his eyes or the fact that, for as much as she was holding on to him, he was doing his best not to touch her in any way. The look on her face was one of pure bliss. I doubted she would stop smiling for a week, which made it difficult to suppress my own smile.

"Are you excited to spend the day with him?" I asked.

"Mom didn't say we would get to meet Levi," she said. "Best surprise ever, Mr. Coach."

"Sounds like it to me. But you can call me Bergy." I dug out my wallet and removed a few bills, then passed them over to my young defenseman. "I've got a few things I have to see to before I can help you out. Take them up to the press box. Show them around, introduce them to whoever they want to meet up there, buy them some snacks and drinks. Just be yourself." Then I thought to add, "But watch your language. I'll be up to join you before everything gets started."

"But…I…"

The kid looked like a lost puppy, to the point I was tempted to pet him. Something told me Sophie might take care of that for me if the idea came to her. I knew better than to be the one to plant the idea in her head.

"You'll be fine," I promised him. "They're just girls. Besides, they've got their mother with them."

Based on what I'd seen so far, I had no doubt Paige Calhoun was the sort of mother who would prevent her daughters from doing anything that would put 501 in harm's way. Even now, she was watching Sophie like a hawk, not that there was anything to worry about. She should be more worried about me and 501 doing something to Sophie, since she didn't know us at all, but her focus was squarely on making sure her daughter didn't do anything she shouldn't.

I understood it better than most. Growing up with a younger sister born with Down syndrome gave me a good grasp on the single-minded determination those kids could have, not to mention the fact that they often missed social cues that other kids would pick up. But I also knew they tended to have hearts of gold.

The thing was, underneath it all, they were just like the rest of us. They were just people, and that meant Sophie was just a girl like any other her age in so many ways. She had hormones and would experience crushes and love and heartache the same as everyone else. And right now? She had the opportunity to spend the whole day with her crush. I'd be damned if I didn't do whatever it took to make it a memorable day for her and her entire family. If I could have done something similar for Linnea when she was this age, I would have done it in a heartbeat.

"You're sure, Bergy?" 501 said, looking at me like I was a madman. And maybe he was right about that. "I mean… This is… I don't—"

"Positive," Sophie responded, despite the fact that he hadn't asked her anything at all. She tightened her grip on him. "You're my date."

I arched a brow and nodded. "I think Sophie's got the right of it." I clapped a hand on 501's shoulder in encouragement and nudged him in the direction of Sophie's mother and sisters. "All right," I said once we were next to them again, unable to stop myself from looking in Paige's direction. Paige's allure was far different from Sophie's but no less magnetic. I needed to watch myself around her. For all I knew, she was married. Even if she wasn't, that meant she was a single mother. Either way, she had a hell of a lot more in her life that needed her focus than me finding her attractive. I smiled for her. Couldn't stop myself, actually. "Looks like you're all set. I'll be up to help out in a bit, but in the meantime, you're in good hands."

The oldest of the daughters looked like she was about to pass out, but she couldn't tear her eyes away from 501. One of the others was having the opposite reaction to being near him, nearly bursting out of her skin with the sort of exuberance and overabundance of energy that could only come from teenage hormones.

But even though her girls certainly drew my eye momentarily, it was Paige who held my attention. She had the most amazing long hair that fell straight down her back, almost pure black in color and as thick and luxurious as I'd ever seen. She was petite and fit, and she seemed to know that she was gorgeous exactly as she was, not bothering with more than a light dusting of makeup.

Her uneasiness over the current situation appeared to be getting the best of her, as she shifted from foot to foot and reached up to resituate the strap of her purse over her shoulder. That action drew my eye to her hand. More specifically, to her ring finger. Which was bare. I wasn't sure why I'd bothered to notice that, but I had. And she saw the recognition hit my face, too, if her sudden blinking was any indication.

But then she shook her head, as if that would be enough to brush whatever was bothering her aside. Her expression was as apologetic as I'd ever seen, which was saying something. My own mother had spent years apologizing for Linnea, even though there'd been no damned good reason to apologize, before she'd finally broken the habit. Something told me Paige hadn't managed that feat yet. She opened her mouth, but I cut her off before she could tell me she was sorry. That was the last thing she needed to say, and I definitely didn't need to hear it.

"My sister has Down syndrome," I said.

I wasn't sure why I told her that other than it was the first thing that came to mind and the only thing that came to my lips in time to stop her apology. And it worked. She snapped her mouth closed, and everything about her appearance changed in an instant. Her hazel eyes softened, and she dropped her hand to her side instead of attempting to force Sophie to release 501's arm.

"Does she?" Paige asked.

Sophie lit up. "You have a sister, Bergy? Where is she? I want to meet her."

I chuckled. "She's in Sweden. I don't think you'll be able to meet her today."

"Okay. Maybe tomorrow."

"I don't know about that," Paige said. "You have to go back to school on Monday."

"Can Levi come to school with me? I want to show him to my friends."

With that, 501 tensed up.

"I bet we can get some pictures to show your friends," I said, and he started breathing again. I glanced at my watch. "But for you, I think you should go have some fun with him."

"Okay," Sophie said. She took off walking in the wrong direction, dragging 501 alongside her. The rest of the Calhouns followed in their wake.

Somehow, 501 must have convinced Sophie that he knew a better way of getting to their ultimate destination, because they turned around and shuffled past me heading in the appropriate direction.

"Give me twenty minutes," I called out as they passed me by.

501 nodded, wide-eyed, but it was Paige's expression that once again drew my eye. She seemed completely and utterly perplexed as her head swiveled so she could take me in.

And now, whether it was a good idea or not, I really wanted to get to know her.

Chapter Two

Paige

IT WASN'T MUCH longer before we were given the royal treatment ten times over. Levi took us up a private elevator and led us through a series of halls we never would have been able to see otherwise. Every now and then, a security guard would ask to see our badges, which Sophie would lift up high in the air and wave around for them, but then they would wave us through. We stopped at a concession stand and Levi bought the girls drinks and snacks—despite my attempt to pay for them myself—before showing us around the press box. He introduced us to the Storm's television crew as well as Axel Johansson and Jiri Dvorak, a couple of other players who, like Levi, were currently injured and ineligible to participate on the ice today.

Now he'd found us all seats together near the front of the box. Axel and Jiri joined us, spreading out between my girls, who giggled and tittered nervously. Well, all of them but Sophie. I'd never seen my youngest so confident. She hadn't released Levi's hand once since she'd first latched on to him, and I was positive I would have to pry her fingers loose later. The poor guy would have to go to the bathroom sometime, at the very least, and she couldn't very well follow him in there. Not that she wouldn't try. I knew her better than to think she would voluntarily release him any time in the next decade. He'd be lucky to find his freedom within a century or two.

I sat down a couple of rows behind them all, close enough to be certain that none of my girls did anything they shouldn't—always a concern, considering the sheer number of hormones wreaking havoc on my household these days—but giving them enough distance so they wouldn't feel as if I were breathing down their necks.

The lights in the arena dimmed, the music cranked up, and the stage lights started to flash. A video came up on the Jumbotron overhead at the same time as I felt someone take a seat next to me.

Based on the hit of expensive cologne that wafted over to me and tickled my nostrils, I had no doubt that *someone* was actually the coach. He smelled good enough to eat, a realization that made my belly flutter like it hadn't done in years. Not since well before Dan and I divorced, actually. The spark had gone out years before we'd given up on the marriage, fading in the strain of countless specialist visits and oodles of therapist appointments that had been necessary for Sophie's development.

They say there aren't many marriages that are strong enough to withstand the strain of raising a special needs child. I now had the firsthand knowledge to be able to say that they, whoever *they* might be, were absolutely one hundred percent right.

But now I had butterflies in my belly for the first

time in well over a decade, and it was because of this man sitting to my left, close enough to me that his body heat melded with my own.

The truth was there simply hadn't been time for attraction or lust or a fling. There hadn't even been time for *me*. All my energy had been put into making sure my daughters had everything they needed, and when I got as close to meeting those needs as I possibly could, I collapsed in a heap and attempted to get what sleep was possible. No matter what, I always felt inadequate and stretched too thin. I worried that I wasn't giving Zoe, Evie, and Izzy the support they needed because I was so fixated on Sophie. I *knew* that no matter how much of my focus I gave Sophie, it wasn't enough. There just wasn't time for any sort of romantic relationship, and if I couldn't make the time to sleep, then I definitely didn't have time for sex. I hadn't even thought about it in years because the simple act of thinking about sex required energy I couldn't muster.

But all of a sudden, being in Mattias Bergstrom's presence had parts of my body coming alive that had long since been dormant, and I couldn't say I minded. At the very least, it served as a good reminder that I was very much still a woman, not just a mother. It was good to know I hadn't completely lost that side of myself.

"I didn't mean to be pushy," he said quietly. The girls and his players were all busy talking and laughing and watching the spectacle below us, so I doubted they would have heard him anyway. "I just thought of my sister when I saw Sophie, and I wanted to give her an experience she wouldn't otherwise be able to have. It was instinct."

"I wasn't positive you recognized you might be stepping on my toes," I said. The fact that he realized he was overstepping, considering we'd only just met, was a point in his favor. Those only seemed to be adding up. I needed to keep an eye on my response to this man before I got myself into trouble. "It's not that I don't appreciate—"

"You don't need to explain."

I glanced over at him and locked on to his blue-gray eyes, which seemed to see straight into my soul, but that was enough to convince me to take him at his word. I seemed to put so much effort into explaining things, because most of the world didn't really understand what Down syndrome was, that it was second nature. It was nice to be around someone who simply understood. I smiled. I couldn't help it.

"I promise I won't offer your girls anything else without talking to you first," Mattias said. The way he looked at me when he said it left me breathless, almost trembling. He might as well have told me I was the most beautiful woman he'd ever seen, because that was what his eyes were saying to me. Those words had a decidedly more profound effect on me than anything he could have said about my appearance might have, anyway.

"Thank you for that." Belatedly, I realized I was staring down at my hands in my lap, my sudden shyness similar to Zoe's when she'd seen her crush across the concourse, and I forced myself to meet his gaze again. Good grief. I was thirty-nine years old. I should be able to look in a man's eyes without falling apart like my teenaged daughter at my age, and I'd be damned if I wouldn't manage it.

He smiled. Heaven help me, he had the most amazing smile. It was bold and confident but nowhere close to being cocky.

"I thought hockey players were supposed to be missing half their teeth," I joked. But then I remembered that he was the coach, not one of the players, and I wished I could take it back. Not that you could tell he wasn't a player based on his size.

He was every inch as big and strong as the three younger men seated in front of us. Maybe even bigger. There was no hiding the muscle filling out his frame, not even under the impeccable suit he wore, and their builds were closer to those of teenaged boys. It took years to build up the kind of muscle mass Mattias had. I knew muscles as well as I knew the back of my hand. I worked with them every day. Even with my eyes closed, I could tell so many things about a person just using my sense of touch.

But Mattias winked. "Now that I'm not playing anymore, I got permanent bridges put in." Then he flashed that smile at me again, not that I could tell the difference between the real teeth or the fake ones.

Yeah. That was a panty-melting smile if ever there was one. Poof! My panties might as well be gone. Which meant my brain had already all but disappeared.

If I had to spend too much time in this man's presence, I was due for some serious trouble.

"So you played before you coached?" I asked, trying to bring everything internal back under control.

"Nearly two decades in the National Hockey League. I grew up playing hockey in Stockholm. My grandparents made a lot of sacrifices so I could play, especially once my sister came into the picture. She needed so much of my parents' time and their resources, it was the only way I would have been able to play."

I didn't know what social services were like in

Sweden, but I knew all too well what they were like here. Dan and I put every penny we could into Sophie's trust. She'd be able to get a job someday, but it wouldn't be the sort of job that would support her. At least she would have her sisters once the two of us were gone, but the more we could have already in place for her, the better.

But, as tempting as it was to talk to him more about his sister, I ended up putting my foot in my mouth again.

"How many teeth did you lose?"

"A dozen?" He gave me an odd look, as if he thought I could confirm or deny his response. "No, maybe it was thirteen."

"That's a lot of teeth to lose."

"Yes, but it was a small price to pay to be able to build the career I had. Actually, the one I have," he corrected himself.

"I suppose you must love hockey. It's nice to be able to make a career out of doing something you love."

"You sound like someone who has experience doing exactly that."

I arched a brow. "Do I?"

"Like recognizes like," he replied, a knowing tone coloring his words.

And he was right. I did love my work. Massage therapy was physically exhausting work but as rewarding as anything I'd ever done outside of being a mother. "I suppose you're right," I finally conceded after he continued to eye me with a hint of a smirk.

"So, tell me, Paige," he said. "Is it all right if I call you Paige?"

"Yes." At the moment, I was fine with him calling me anything, as long as he would keep talking. He had a smooth, rich voice, and the hint of his Swedish accent was just enough to present some spice, like chocolate with a hint of cinnamon.

"Paige. I like that name. You can call me Matti if you want."

"Matti? Is that what everyone calls you?"

"Not everyone," he said. "Just my sister. But you can call me that if it fits for you."

"Oh." The word came out sounding soft and dreamy. Sitting here and talking with him made me *feel* soft and dreamy. But he didn't look like a Matti to me. He seemed much too dignified for that. Too hot. "I think I'll stick with Mattias, if you don't mind."

"I don't mind." The corners of his eyes crinkled. It didn't make him look old, just insanely handsome. "Tell me what it is you love to do, Paige."

I didn't even pause to think. Before I could stop myself, I said, "To look at you." I could have shot myself for blurting that out, but there was no taking it back.

And there was no deluding myself into thinking he might have missed it, either. Not with the way he chuckled. "I love to look at you, too," Mattias said. "I think I'm enjoying it a lot more than I should."

I should have kept my mouth shut. I should have turned to check on my girls, or looked to see what was happening down on the ice, or done any number of things other than what I did next. But, just like the teenager in a thirty-nine-year-old's body I'd apparently become, I did the exact opposite of what I should do; I let my hormones win.

"Why shouldn't you enjoy looking?" I asked, sounding much saucier than I felt. Inside, everything was roiling and jumbling and taut, like Izzy's bowstring during archery practice.

Mattias angled his head, taking me in more fully. Not to mention appreciatively. "Well, if you put it that way."

Not only had I put it that way but I didn't want to take it back, as long as he was going to continue looking at me that way.

It had been too damn long since anyone had flirted with me. I wasn't fooling myself. This wasn't going to last any longer than just today, but that didn't mean I couldn't enjoy myself for a little while.

It wouldn't mean the world was ending.

No harm would come to my girls just because I decided to let myself feel like a woman for a few hours.

Maybe a little flirtation was exactly what the doctor ordered. After today, life could go back to normal. But for now? A sexy-as-sin man was looking at me like there was nothing else he would rather be doing, nowhere else he would rather be, and I was determined to let myself enjoy it.

I COULDN'T SEEM to help myself. I'd initially been drawn to Sophie, but now that she was happily latched on to 501 for the foreseeable future, her mother was drawing all my focus.

She was blinking at me. I couldn't decide if she was wishing she hadn't returned my flirtation or surprised that she had. Either way, I didn't mind. I liked the effect I seemed to be having on Paige. In fact, I might like it a bit too much. Wedding ring or no, she probably didn't have time to get involved with someone, let alone a man as married to his work as me. It had always been my biggest flaw. I couldn't keep track of how many times Linnea had told me to *Loosen up, Matti*. I worked so hard in order to be sure she never went without anything and everything she needed, of course, but Linnea never saw that. She only knew she rarely got to see me other than on a TV screen and for a few weeks in the summer, which wasn't nearly enough.

I'd thought about bringing her to the US with me. In fact, I'd talked it over with our parents multiple times, but we'd always concluded it was best to keep her in Sweden. While she was there, she had our parents, she had her friends, she knew the language, and she was receiving excellent social services. If I brought her to live with me, we would have to go through a mountain of paperwork and red tape to get her the same benefits, and then what would happen if I ended up working for a team in Canada instead of the States? It was a definite possibility, so we'd decided to keep Linnea in Sweden as long as our parents were able to continue giving her the aid she needed. After that, I'd have some tough decisions to make.

That was yet another reason for me to avoid getting involved with someone. In fact, I'd sworn off starting up new relationships with women years ago. I'd dated a few women back in my playing days, but it had never lasted long. They didn't understand why I chose to live modestly, driving a Toyota instead of a Mercedes and living in a reasonable house instead of buying a multimillion-dollar house. They were gold diggers, plain and simple. They wanted me to spend lavishly on them, and when I refused—stating I had other, more important uses for my money—things came crashing to a halt. After a few repetitions of this same pattern, I'd decided it wasn't worth my while to keep putting myself through it, and it definitely wasn't worth potentially losing anything I intended to set aside for Linnea's future.

Something told me Paige would more than understand where I was coming from, which only encouraged me to keep up the flirtation we'd already started. This might not be my brightest move ever, but I couldn't seem to stop myself.

The blaring music from the opening of the event finally came to an end, and they brought up the lights again. The team was split in half, one group wearing the home colors and the other group wearing road whites. As captain, Babs had made the executive decision as to who would be coaching each of the two teams today. He'd brought in kids from some of the local peewee teams to take over that job, giving me and the rest of the coaches the day off, essentially. Tim Whitlock, the Storm's in-arena entertainment director, came over the PA system to announce the first event would be the fastest skater competition.

"Fastest skater," Paige murmured. "Any chance this would have been your event?"

"Not in this lifetime. Skating was never my strength." I'd been lucky to make it into the NHL at all, actually, but I'd found ways to make my shortcomings work for me. "I would have been in the hardest shot competition."

She passed appraising eyes over me, letting them hold longer than necessary on my biceps. "I suppose I can see that."

"This should be interesting, though. The whole team right now is built on speed and skill, other than a couple of the older veteran players. There are a few guys who are faster than others, of course, but I think the winner could surprise some people."

"My money's on Jens," 501 said, looking over his shoulder at us.

"Jens?" Jo-Jo said incredulously. "Not a chance. It's Koz all the way."

Devo let out a cross between a snort and a chuckle. "Coop young and fast. Too big energy. He leave them in dust." His English was broken and heavy with his Eastern European accent, but there he got his point across well enough.

The three they named were certainly among the top contenders, but I had someone else in mind who could potentially run away with it. I thought Nate "Ghost" Golston had an opportunity to make a big impression today.

Paige's daughters tittered and giggled, each of them naming a player she thought was the fastest. They still hadn't settled down by the time the competition began.

After the two goalies raced each other in full pads—which was a complete debacle but got the fans involved when Nicky just barely beat Bobby by a skate blade—they ran five heats of regular skaters. In the end, it was Ghost for the white team and Koz for the purple team who turned in the fastest times. They were all set to race each other to determine the winner when Paige leaned over.

"You don't seem at all surprised," she said quietly in my ear. Her breath tickled my neck, turning my thoughts entirely away from the action down below.

"Ghost was my pick from the beginning," I said.

"Ghost was? Really?" 501 gave me a look of pure skepticism.

"Yeah, Ghost. Maybe you should think about why

that is." Ghost was easily the smallest guy on the team, so a lot of times he got overlooked by guys like 501 and other defensemen like him. They thought that because they had longer legs and weighed more, they would have the upper hand. I knew from experience, though, that the smallest guys out there were also the best at evading the big guys like me, and it had a lot to do with speed. When Ghost wanted to turn on his jets, he could really fly across the ice. I hoped he would choose to do so today, actually. I wanted to use it to convince him he could give more than he'd been giving in games in order to be a more effective player.

I'd never been the kind of teacher who would spell everything out for someone, though. I liked letting my players learn things on their own, only giving them a nudge in the right direction when necessary. That was what I hoped to do with 501. He let out a grunting sort of sound and turned his attention back to the ice, while the crew changed the setup for the next event.

"I bet you would win," Sophie said adoringly to him.

"Not likely," Jo-Jo said. "501 would trip and slam headfirst into the goal post again or something." Which was exactly how my young defenseman had ended up with concussion symptoms. It was worse than that, even. Somehow, he'd gotten himself called for a tripping penalty in the process of chasing the opposing player back to the goal, and he'd almost knocked the puck into our net at the same time.

The boys had been giving him shit over it ever since.

The coaches and I had been, too, to be honest, but in a different way. We'd been using this time while he was forced to sit out to remind him to slow down and that he had more time to make his moves than he seemed to think. Sometimes, it was better to take a step back, especially for a young guy like him. Being up here right now might not be fun for him, but it was far better for his future in the league.

Sophie didn't pay Jo-Jo any attention. Her eyes were only for 501. "You would win," she repeated.

One of her sisters, who had previously been just as smitten with 501 as Sophie, was now making gaga eyes at Jo-Jo, though.

I said a silent prayer that all my players would remember that these were teenaged girls and, therefore, well out of bounds. Then I chuckled and got up to get a drink, nodding at my assistant coaches, David Weber and Adam Hancock, as I passed them. I'd barely gotten to the back of the room, where we had a buffet table full of drinks, sandwich fixings, and the like, when Paige caught me, stopping so close she almost brushed up against me.

She smelled like sunshine—warmth and fresh air combining into a state of perfection. I'd noticed it earlier, but it nearly knocked me on my ass now. "Can I get you something?" I asked. I should have asked her before I got up to begin with. I just hadn't been thinking.

She shook her head. "I just wanted… I wanted to thank you. It's really rare that anyone thinks to do anything for Sophie, let alone for the rest of my girls. I wanted you to know how much I appreciate it."

"I only did what anyone would do," I said, but even as the words left my mouth, I knew them to be untrue. She was right. Most people wouldn't have done what I had, whether they had the opportunity to do it or not. They would look right past this young girl, assuming that they'd offend by offering help where it wasn't wanted or simply not having a clue what help they should offer. Too many times, I'd seen people completely look past Linnea, ignoring her or pretending they didn't see her. And it always made me mad. It made me feel inadequate, because no matter how big or strong I was and no matter how much money I made, I couldn't protect her from the cruelty she'd faced every day of her life, whether she recognized it as what it was or not. It made me hurt for my sister, who was so sweet and always thought the best of everyone she came into contact with, whether they deserved her sweetness or not.

People apologized when I confronted them about it. They were always quick to make excuses. They just didn't realize they were making assumptions about her, whether they recognized it or not. They assumed Linnea was less than they were. They assumed she wouldn't fit in or couldn't do what they were going to do. They made plenty of assumptions.

Because of that, the only thing I would ever assume about Sophie was that she would most likely surprise me at every turn.

"I suppose that's not exactly true, is it?" I said, once again letting a slight grin creep to my lips. I couldn't seem to help that when it came to Sophie, the same as when I was with Linnea. The surprising thing was that Paige was starting to have a similar effect on me.

"No." The look in Paige's eyes was one I couldn't quite place. Curiosity, maybe? "No, it's not the case. Far from it. So thank you. It means more to me than you could ever know."

"I think I do know," I said. "If someone had done something like this for my sister, I would have done anything I could to be sure they understood what it meant to me. But regardless of what anyone else would do, I felt it was only right."

She didn't say anything, picking up a small dessert plate and putting a few grapes and bits of pineapple on it. My eye once again fell to her hand. Still no wedding ring, not that I'd expected one to appear out of thin air.

"So if there's anything else I can do for Sophie, anything you and your husband can think of…" I intentionally left the suggestion hanging in the air, waiting to see if she'd answer the question that was eating me alive.

"My ex-husband, you mean." Not only did she answer me but her eyes fluttered up to meet mine. She was flirting with me as much as I was flirting with her.

I had to hold myself back from doing a victory dance. That wouldn't be appreciated right now. "Your ex," I repeated after her. "Just let me know."

"Why are you doing this?" Paige asked, popping a grape in her mouth. "Are you really just a good guy, and this is exactly what you say—that you were drawn to Sophie because she reminds you of your sister, and that's it? Nothing more?"

"There might be something more." Fuck, it had been a long time since I'd tried to banter with a woman I was interested in. I was seriously out of practice. With everything else I did in life, I had all the confidence in the world. I knew what I was doing every step of the way before beginning step one, and I never stumbled or fumbled my way through it. But with this? I felt like a gangly fourteen-year-old boy again, with feet that had grown faster than the rest of me that had me tripping over them with every step I took. "There is something more," I corrected myself.

"Which is?" She picked up a napkin and folded it, slipping it beneath her plate.

"The truth is, I'm drawn to you every bit as much as I'm drawn to your daughter," I forced out. "I want to get to know you, Paige."

A smile crept to her lips despite her obvious effort to keep it at bay. "I'm not sure how I feel about that."

And that was as good as a punch in the gut—further proof that she already had her hands full without adding a man like me to it. I had no business chasing after this single mother, and I knew it, but damn if I didn't want to convince her it was a good idea.

Then, picking up a glass of water, she turned to go back to her seat.

I put a hand on her shoulder, stopping her, before I could think through what I was doing. In fact, I didn't want to think it through. I'd acted without planning every tiny detail when I'd invited her and her daughters to join us for the day, and so far it had turned out better than I could have imagined even if I was faltering at every turn. Maybe I needed to be spontaneous more often. Maybe it would be good for me.

Maybe Paige would be good for me. And maybe I could be good for her.

She glanced up at me, her brow arched. "Yes?"

"Do you and your girls have plans tomorrow?" I asked. Her lips formed a perfect O, but she didn't immediately turn me down, so I pushed through. "It's still the weekend. We've got an afternoon game. I'd like you to come as my guests. If you want. And if you don't have other plans. We could maybe have dinner after."

"I…" She looked as lost as she sounded, as if she was as out of practice was I was.

But then one of her girls—probably the oldest one—came over to the buffet table and started fixing herself a plate. She glanced up at me. "Did you just ask my mom out on a date?"

"I did." I kept my eyes on Paige while I answered her daughter.

"What she means to say is *yes*. And by the way, she likes tulips. Yellow ones."

"*Zoe*," Paige said in a very mom-like voice.

"What? You do like tulips." Zoe gave me a cheeky grin. "Can we hang out with 501 during the game?"

Chapter Three

Paige

WITH MATTIAS'S HELP, I managed to extricate Levi from Sophie's exuberant grip and guide all of my girls toward the parking garage after the StormSkillz event came to a close. Mattias came with us, actually, walking along beside me while my daughters raced ahead in a torrent of squeals pitched so high that only a dog should be able to hear them.

"You think they had a good time?" he asked me, the deep rumble of his voice a pleasing contrast to their excited chatter.

I chuckled. "I doubt they'll stop talking about it for a month." Even as I said it, Sophie turned her head to look at us over her shoulder, her smile as sweet as I'd ever seen it. Her eyes were all crinkled up, and her cheeks were flushed with exhilaration. She looked like she might never be able to stop smiling.

"That's good."

"Good, yes, but they might drive me insane with it before the month is out." In a good way, though.

Sometimes I complained about how excitable they could be when it came to boys and their crushes, but really I wouldn't change it for anything.

"I guess I'll have to make that up to you," he said, and my butterflies returned.

They kept coming back, each instance stronger than the last, when he did even the smallest thing. Sometimes it was when he would smile at me with that panty-melting look in his eye. Once, they'd fluttered to life when he'd entertained Sophie while Levi escaped for a few minutes, answering every question she put to him as though it was the most important question he'd ever heard. Another time, the flutters caught me unawares when he took the time to explain what icing was to Izzy.

How pathetic was it that this man could turn me on simply by taking an interest in my daughters? But it was the truth. He'd paid as much attention to each of the four of them as he had to me over the course of the afternoon, and he'd even taken a few moments to talk to his players and give them instruction for their own play based on some of the games and drills taking place on the ice below us. If I wasn't careful, I might find myself falling for this man, and that wasn't something that fit well in my plans.

"They're growing up too fast for me," I admitted. "When they were little, there were times I couldn't wait for them to grow up. Three was always a rough year. Whoever decided the twos were terrible must never have met a three-year-old. I didn't think I would escape their threes with all of us being alive and intact."

Mattias chuckled. "But here you are."

"But here we are, and they're teenagers. I think I blinked one day and they were practically adults. Now I regret all those moments I wished they would hurry past those difficult stages, and I'm praying they'll slow down."

"Sadly, I don't think it works that way."

"No, it doesn't." I glanced up at him and caught him staring at me in the way he had that made my heart race, and I quickly looked ahead again. "What about you?" I asked to deflect my own attention away from the overwhelming *awareness* he brought out in me. "Do you have kids growing up too fast? Or maybe already grown?"

"No kids. Just my sister." His arm brushed against mine, and I broke out in gooseflesh. He didn't react to the contact. "Linnea has a boyfriend, my mother tells me. He's got DS, too. He works in the mail room with her and asked her out for ice cream after work one day. Now they're talking about how they want to live together."

"Oh, wow. Have you met him?"

"Many times. They've worked together for years. They've been friends for a long time."

"And do you like him?"

"As a man? Sure. As a man my sister is living with?" He laughed and shook his head. "It's hard to wrap my head around it, is all."

Since the thought of Sophie dating someone gave me hives, I could understand that. "Has she dated before?"

"There was one," he said cautiously, making me wonder what had happened with that first boyfriend. "It's been a while, though. And I want her to be happy and have love in her life, but I can't help but worry. I mean, it was only a few years ago that she moved out of my parents' house to live in a group home."

"But she's done that," I said. "And she's fine. Right? She has a job. He does, too. You don't think he's trying to take advantage of her, do you?"

"No, it's nothing like that," he rushed to say. "I just never thought she would live on her own, let alone with a man. She keeps surprising me. In good ways."

The girls were already halfway down the escalator. Mattias put his hand on the small of my back as I stepped onto it in a slightly protective yet somewhat possessive move, and I had to fight the urge not to inch closer to him.

I swallowed hard. "Sophie surprises me every day," I forced past my thick tongue. "In good ways, too. She's exactly like her sisters in some ways."

"Like with having a crush on 501," he said, chuckling. He was on the step directly behind me, his body heat warming my backside.

"Yes, like that." I spun so I could see him, but looking up at his face, with him being a step above me, left me dizzy.

He tightened his grip on my waist, steadying me, but that didn't stop me from reaching out to grab on to him, as well, my hands resting on his torso. My fingers could feel every single muscle underneath them. Six-pack? He probably had eight. He was solid and unmovable, and my knees were weak.

"You all right?" he asked.

I was fine except for the fact that I might have a crush on Mattias Bergstrom even bigger than all the girls' crushes on Levi Babcock combined. The way he was holding me upright, acting as if I were as light as a feather and it was simply what anyone would do, robbed me of all thought. Including my purpose in turning around to look at him to begin with. All I could do was hold on and hope he didn't care that I was suddenly sixteen again.

"Fine," I finally managed to breathe.

"Fine enough to walk? Because we're almost to the bottom." He laughed, but not in a way that made me feel as though he were laughing *at* me.

I turned around and managed to step off the escalator without tripping over my own feet, but that wasn't saying a whole lot. Mattias kept an arm around my waist, and I was happy for him to leave it there.

We didn't say anything the rest of the way to the parking garage. The girls were huddled together by my SUV when we got there, still giggling and chattering so much I doubted they'd settle down before midnight at the very earliest. There wasn't a chance they'd let me get much sleep tonight. Add to that my nerves about this supposed date with Mattias tomorrow…

Sophie spun around and headed our way, arms outstretched. I thought she was coming to hug me, so I opened up to accept it. I wasn't her target, though. She walked straight into Mattias's arms and gave him a bear hug. He gave back as good as he got, even lifting her off her feet and swinging her around while she giggled. His smile was as wide as hers.

And that was it. I was a goner. There wasn't any chance I would be able to stop myself from falling for this man. I didn't know him very well yet, but in these few hours, he'd shown me everything I needed to know.

My eyes stung, and I put a hand up to cover my mouth, as if that would be enough to stop me from crying. Not that there was any realistic chance of that happening.

"Thank you, Bergy," she said when he set her back

on the ground.

He winked and took a knee, dropping down to be on her level. "You're welcome, Sophie."

Zoe dug a tissue out of her purse and brought it over to me. I wiped my eyes with it but gave up after a few tears. They weren't going to stop any time soon if Mattias kept being this sweet with my baby.

"Can I meet your sister someday?"

"Maybe," he said. "We'll have to see if we can work that out."

"How come she can't just come over to my house?"

"Well, she lives a long way away."

I heard a sniffle and glanced over to my other girls. They were all three crying, just like I was. I made a mental snapshot of this moment, not wanting to let it slip away too soon.

"How far?" Sophie asked, turning the palms of her hands up and shrugging. "She could come over tomorrow. Mom won't mind."

"Halfway around the world."

Her eyes went wide. "That's a *long* way, Bergy. Maybe she can come on Friday."

He laughed and said, "Maybe. I'll have to see what I can work out."

"I need you to help me," she said, her tone as serious as it ever was. I didn't know what she was about to ask him for, but I started mentally preparing myself to dig him out of whatever hole she tried to drag him into. I knew this tone of voice, and she wasn't going to give up on whatever it might be very easily. In fact, I was afraid it had something to do with a certain young man named Levi.

"If it's something that's okay with your mother and something I can help you with, I promise you I will."

And he sounded as sincere as she was determined.

"I want to play hockey like Levi. I want to skate fast."

Instantly, my mind started turning over every reason I'd ever been told she'd never be able to do X, Y, or Z. From the moment my OB-GYN had told us that my unborn baby had Down syndrome, they'd been trying to pound into my brain all the things she couldn't do. Things she would *never* be able to do, no matter how much she wanted to and no matter how hard she tried.

I'd never fallen into the trap of letting those impossibilities become reality. I'd always encouraged Sophie to follow her heart, to try to do anything she wanted to do. Dan and I both had spent eleven years telling her she could do whatever she wanted if she just tried hard enough, and we'd held her hand through it all. We'd taught her sisters to treat her exactly the same way we did because letting her believe she *couldn't* do something would simply prove it true.

Sophie had participated in the school choir even though they'd told her she couldn't sing. She'd run in track meets even though they'd told her she was too slow. She'd learned to read—albeit at a level far lower than her actual age—even though they'd told her she would never do more than learn the alphabet, if that. She'd proven them wrong so many times, and I knew she would many more. But this time, as her mother, I was afraid.

I was afraid they were right. And I was afraid that she would try, and fail, and try, and fail, and try, and fail…and maybe, eventually, she would just stop trying altogether. And it broke my heart.

Skating, the act of keeping herself upright on those tiny blades… I didn't see how it could be possible.

The older girls' sniffles got louder, and I knew they were thinking along the same lines I was. None of us wanted to see Sophie hurt, but we also didn't want to fall into the trap of telling her she *couldn't*, because we'd always told her she *could*.

Mattias didn't pay our crying any mind. He focused in on Sophie, his expression serious. And he nodded, which made something in my belly flip even as I wanted to stop him from saying whatever was about to come out of his mouth. "You want to skate? To play hockey? That's what you really want?"

"Yes. Just like Levi."

"All right," he said, and my heart sank down lower than my toes, because no matter how much I tried to convince myself that Sophie could do anything she set her mind on, I knew it wasn't really true. And skating? Playing hockey? That would be as close to impossible a task as she could set for herself. But Mattias didn't let it deter him, and I didn't stop him in time to prevent him from making her a promise that he would never be able to keep. "I'll make you a deal."

"What deal?"

"You convince your mom to let me kiss her after our date tomorrow, and I'll find a way to make it happen. I'll help you learn to skate and play hockey. It might take longer than tomorrow, though."

"Deal!" Sophie said.

Done. That was that, even though I knew she was in for a huge disappointment when he couldn't find a way to make it possible for her. The balance necessary to stay upright on skate blades, the coordination required to stay on skates while attempting to hit a puck with a stick were outside the realm of her skill set, no matter how much she wanted it and no matter how hard she tried. Whether I was ready for it or not, my sweet little girl was going to try to skate.

And apparently, I was getting a kiss tomorrow.

Mattias

I'D GIVEN THAT little girl a promise I wasn't at all positive I could deliver on, but I'd be damned if I didn't exhaust every resource I had before admitting defeat. And not just because I wanted to kiss her mother, either. I was reasonably certain I'd be able to get the kiss from Paige whether I helped Sophie learn to skate or not.

Playing hockey was something that Linnea had wanted, too, and I'd never been able to give it to her. I had always felt like a failure on that score, like I'd let my sister down. But if I could make it happen for Sophie, taking into account all the technological advances that had taken place in the last few decades and with the hockey minds involved with the Storm organization at my disposal, then maybe I could make it up to Linnea in some way.

Yes, it was an illogical thought, but I didn't care. I was determined to find a way for Sophie Calhoun to learn how to skate and play hockey. And when I made up my mind to do something, there was nothing that would stop me from reaching my goal. I might have some stops and starts. There would likely be failures along the way. But I would only truly fail when I gave up and admitted defeat.

The next morning, well before any of my players were due to arrive, I was already holed up in my office with my laptop open, Googling everything under the moon remotely related to assistive devices for skating to get my ideas flowing. I needed something that would help her stay upright but which would leave her arms free so she could hold a stick, and so far I was coming up empty. I kept coming to devices similar to a walker only with skis on the bottom, but she would have to hold on to something like that with both hands.

David Weber, one of my assistant coaches, poked his head through the door after I'd been working for well over an hour. "Wasn't expecting you here so early," he said. He came in carrying two cups of coffee and set one of them in front of me. "This have anything to do with your hot mom from yesterday?"

I shot him a go-to-hell look. "Her daughter, actually. Sophie wants to skate and play hockey."

"Sophie is the one with Down syndrome?"

I nodded, scrolling through page after page of search results, paying more attention to my computer than I was to him.

Webs gave a grunt of some sort, sounding as sober as I'd ever heard him. That moment of seriousness didn't last long; in no time, he snorted out a laugh. "You could find a way to strap her to 501's legs so he would be doing all the work. Wouldn't hurt him any. Probably be good for him."

"Not going to happen." I wouldn't put 501 through that, and I didn't think Paige would go for it, anyway. "Besides, Doc hasn't cleared 501 for anything physical yet."

"You planning on having him do it today?" Webs demanded. "It'll take us at least a week or more to set up the rig."

"Not today, no. Doesn't matter. That's not the

solution I'm looking for."

Adam "Handy" Hancock came through the door, tossing his gym bag on the floor along the wall. He raised a brow. "What kind of solution do you think you'll find that's better than that?"

I supposed he'd heard quite a bit of our conversation. Either that or it wasn't too difficult to interpret.

"I'm going to find a way for her to do it on her own," I said. I needed to find something that would let Sophie do all the work but give her support while she built up her core strength. If she was serious about it and really worked hard, she could probably eventually skate on her own, but I wanted to know she'd be safe while she worked on getting there.

And while she was working on that, I could work on finding a hockey program she could participate in, one for kids with special needs and developmental difficulties. I knew they existed. I just wasn't sure if there were any of them around Portland. If there were, I would find them and do whatever it took to get her involved.

Webs plopped down in a chair across from me and dug out his iPad, propping it up across from me. "Sounds like you've got it bad."

I glanced up from my screen again. He was giving me a knowing look, the sort that said he knew exactly what was behind my actions, and he assumed it had everything to do with Paige and not her daughter. "I'm not denying that I'm very interested in Paige Calhoun—"

"Good," Handy said, doing the same thing Webs had just done. "Because we'd see straight through it."

"But," I added with a hell of a lot of emphasis,

"that's not why I'm doing this." Not that they needed to know about Linnea. I'd played in the NHL for twenty years and had been coaching ever since, and not once had I said a word about my sister to any of my teammates or coworkers. I wasn't ashamed of her. Far from it. In all honesty, it had a hell of a lot more to do with not wanting anyone to see what I was like with her.

Around the league, I had always been known as a hard-assed son of a bitch. In my playing days, I'd been a big, skilled defenseman with a mean streak. These days, I was a sullen coach with a crusty exterior, more likely to grumble and grouse than to crack a smile. My sister, on the other hand, was all sweetness and light. Simply thinking about her or talking about her was all it took to put a grin on my face and melt away the façade. No one but Linnea needed to see that side of me, or so I had thought until little Sophie had leaped into 501's arms yesterday. That was all it had taken to chip away at my crunchy exterior in front of people I'd never let see that part of my makeup.

And now, here I was. At the moment, I didn't care how many of them had seen my smiles. I didn't give a damn who had noticed the cracks in my armor. All I wanted to do was make one of Sophie's dreams come true.

My two assistant coaches nodded and grunted their assent, but it was clear from the look that passed between them that they weren't buying my denial. Which was probably for the best. Let them think it was all about Paige if that was what they wanted. Maybe that way no one would realize the truth, and I could go on being the hard-ass they'd all come to expect.

We all fell quiet then. They were probably watching

film from the Flames' last game, since we were scheduled to play them this afternoon, or otherwise preparing to do their jobs. Unlike me. I never shirked my responsibilities, but I supposed everyone got a free pass for that every now and then. I'd be ready for the game whether I watched more film or not.

After a few minutes, Webs shot his head up. "What if we could fashion something ourselves?"

"Like a walker on skis that we could strap her into so she wouldn't have to hold on to it," Handy said. He was squinting at his screen, reading something. Not watching film.

Neither of them were watching footage. They were both doing the same damn thing I was, and now Jim Sutter and Drywall Tierney—our GM and the head equipment manager—were coming into my office as well.

Webs nodded, eyes narrowed in thought. "If we set it up to be behind her, she'd have full use of her arms and legs. We could make some sort of harness like you'd use for zip-lining or parachuting."

"Would a walker be sturdy enough if her legs couldn't support her on skates?" Jim asked, crossing his arms and legs and leaning back against the wall.

"It would if I built it," Drywall said.

Before I knew what was happening, half the team executives were gathered in my office, and we were brainstorming ways to help Sophie Calhoun skate.

I still didn't know how we were going to make it happen, but that didn't matter.

Because we were going to make it happen.

Chapter Four

Mattias

NOT WANTING TO keep Paige and her girls waiting any longer than necessary, I headed up to the owner's box at the Moda Center as soon as I'd released the team after the game. We'd won, but it hadn't been easy. The Flames were a young, exciting, well-coached team. There'd been a lot of back-and-forth action and way too many turnovers on both ends of the ice, but my boys had pulled through in the end.

I'd decided to give them a light, optional practice tomorrow. We were already through the first half of the season or so, and things were running along well. There wasn't any need to reinforce systems or anything like that, and we had several guys who had been playing through injuries for a while—Cam "Jonny" Johnson and Grant Wheelan, in particular. A couple more had come off the ice with minor issues in the course of the game, too. It would be better for all of them to get some rest, take maintenance days, so they'd be ready for the grueling push toward the playoffs.

But now, I was gathering up Paige and her daughters for our *date*, if you could call it that. I wasn't positive that I would, but I hadn't been on a real date in years. Did it count if you had four giggling teenaged girls with you? Probably not, but I wasn't going to argue with it.

Sophie was the first to see me when I came through the door. She lit up like a Christmas tree, her smile as wide as I'd ever seen it when 501 wasn't in the room. "Bergy, we *won!*"

"We sure did," I said, holding up my hand for the high five she ran over to give me.

She and her sisters had been sitting with some of the older kids among the players' families. It didn't surprise me at all to find Maddie Campbell, Rachel's oldest daughter, right in the center of them. Rachel was Jim's assistant and the wife of one of my players, Brenden "Soupy" Campbell, who had been out with an injury nearly all season long. Maddie tended to be quiet but perceptive and incredibly thoughtful. She gravitated toward the damaged and the broken, or anyone who needed an extra dose of compassion. Not that Sophie was broken, but it warmed my heart to know that Soupy's shy, sweet girl would have taken Sophie under her wing with all the strangers around.

Paige gathered up the other three and brought them our way in time to hear Sophie ask, "Can Levi come on our date, too?"

"I think Levi has other things he needs to do," Paige answered before I had the chance.

Izzy deflated like a balloon, and Evie's disappointment was tangible. Zoe looked so relieved I almost laughed.

"You don't want him to come?" I asked the oldest girl.

"Nope." Zoe shook her head vigorously. "I turn stupid the second I get near him. I don't think I said more than three words all day yesterday."

"Oh, you said *plenty* once we got home," Paige said, laughing.

"Well, I had to make up for all the time I couldn't speak at all!"

"I don't think you need to have any fear you'll forget how your tongue works," Evie said, giggling. Then she took off out the door, and the rest of us followed behind her, all three of the older girls taking jabs at each other and laughing at such a high pitch that I thought I might lose my hearing if I spent too much time around them. Sophie rushed to keep up with them, once more leaving Paige and me trailing in their wake.

"You've given them quite a weekend," she said after a reasonable distance fell between us and the girls. "I don't think they'll stop talking about it for quite some time."

"I'm glad." More than glad. I might not know these girls very well, let alone their mother, but there was something about being with them that felt *right*, in a way that few things in my life ever had.

"Are you sure you know what you're getting into with this?" Paige waved a hand in front of us, indicating the girls who seemed to be skipping across the air rather than walking. "You can still back out of taking us all to dinner, you know. I'll find a good excuse."

I glanced over at her, taking in the long stretch of her neck. She had her hair all piled on top of her head today, in a sort of bun that looked at once haphazard and elegant.

"Are you trying to get out of that kiss? Because I'm doing everything in my power to follow through with my end of the bargain."

"No!" She looked down at my chest instead of meeting my eyes, though, and I got the distinct sense she was fighting a blush. "No, a deal is a deal."

There was no denying the boost my ego got over the fact that she wasn't telling me to go to hell. But still… "I made that deal with Sophie, not with you. And her part of it was simply to *try* to get you to agree."

"Mattias, she's never going to be—"

"Don't tell me that she won't ever be able to skate. Not you. Not her mother." Even as the words left my mouth, I had to wonder if I meant them more for Paige in dealing with Sophie or if I was thinking of my own mother and Linnea. Either way, I meant it.

"But the kind of balance that would require? The strength to keep herself up on those blades?" The same worried look Paige had taken on last night when I'd first talked with Sophie came back into her eyes now. "I just don't want to see her fail so many times that she stops trying. I don't want to see her give up."

"What if she doesn't give up? What if she doesn't stop trying?" I argued.

"But—"

"I can't promise that she'll ever be able to do it on her own, but what's the harm in trying? Technology has advanced so much in recent years. I think I can find a way to at least get her out on the ice, and then we can see what happens. If we can devise something to help her balance at first, there's no telling what she'll be able to do down the line."

"You're talking like you're still going to be involved when it gets to that," Paige said, frustration punctuating her words.

"And you're talking like I won't be."

She stopped cold, and I had to stop, too, or I'd completely pass her by.

"Look, Mattias," she said, using the same tone my mother had always used when she was trying to protect Linnea as best she could. "I know you mean well. I do. And I appreciate it more than I could ever say."

"But?" There was no point trying to hide from it, since we both knew the *but* was coming.

"*But* you and me? We're adults. We can handle disappointment. We understand that you're a good man trying to do something nice for my little girl, but you're probably getting yourself in deeper than you initially intended. You probably didn't realize all of the implications of what you were suggesting. Maybe you do now. I hope so, at least. But Sophie doesn't always understand when people back away. She gets attached, and then they leave before they're able to keep their promises, and then she gets hurt. And my girls and I are the ones left to pick up the pieces. We're the ones who have to listen to her ask, over and over again, where Dad is and why he isn't with us, or why her friends stopped coming to play, or why she isn't able to move on to the next grade in school when all her friends are."

"So what are you saying?" I asked cautiously. Although I probably didn't really need to ask. I could tell where she was going with this. She was trying to kick me out before I got too close, before my leaving could hurt too much.

Maybe she was right to do that. Not because I wouldn't follow through with helping Sophie learn to play hockey but because there wasn't a ton of job security as a coach in the NHL, and I had responsibilities to take care of in Sweden. I had to go wherever the work took me, and that might mean stepping out of Sophie's life at some point down the line.

Paige put her arms over her chest in a self-protective gesture. No matter how big a game she talked, I could see through it. She wasn't just trying to protect Sophie in all this.

"I'm saying," she said after a protracted silence, "maybe it's for the best if you step away after tonight. She hasn't latched on to you too much yet. You're still just in the *maybe we can find a way to make this work* phase. You haven't yet made her any official promises that you'll have to break eventually."

"Why would I have to break them?" I asked, even though I knew all the answers she would likely come up with, and then some that wouldn't even cross Paige's mind. But she didn't know me very well yet. She didn't know that I was the most determined son of a bitch she'd ever met. She didn't know that once I set a goal for myself, there would be no stopping me. Now I needed to make her understand, or at the very least give her a hint.

She was looking at me like trees were sprouting from my ears.

I raised a brow. "Like you said, a deal is a deal. I told Sophie I would do whatever I could to help her out. I meant it."

The corners of Paige's lips quirked up, despite her efforts to fight off the smile. "I'd let you kiss me even if you didn't hold up your end of it," she said. Then she bit her lower lip, and I couldn't look anywhere else.

"And why would you do that?"

She shrugged. "Because it's been too long."

It'd been too long for both of us, then.

"Mom!" Zoe shouted from well ahead of us, and

Paige whipped her head in that direction. "You can kiss him later. We're hungry." We were too far away to see it, but an eye roll was overly evident in Zoe's tone.

Paige pressed her eyes closed for a moment before glancing up to meet my eyes. She pinched her lips together in a thin line, and a gorgeous blush stole over her cheeks. "Sorry. We should— We should go." Then she took off heading toward her daughters with a determined stride.

I turned to keep up with her. Reaching out to put a hand on the small of her back, I tried not to laugh. At least not too much. "It's fine. Don't want to keep them waiting."

Once we caught up with the girls, Sophie reached for my free hand. I let her take it, my other hand settling into the curve over her mother's hip while the older girls rolled their eyes and hurried ahead of us...giggling and snickering as they went. They kept peeking over their shoulders at us, though, nearly tripping over their own feet because they weren't paying attention to where they were going.

And it felt good. I only hoped Paige liked it as much as I did. Because, now that I realized how much I enjoyed spending time with her and her girls, I didn't simply intend to follow through with my promise to Sophie; I was starting to think of ways I could make other promises, as well.

MATTIAS HAD TO be bored out of his mind. He'd brought us to the Old Spaghetti Factory for dinner.

Since it was a Sunday evening and we were a party of six, we'd had to wait almost an hour before they had a table big enough to seat all of us together. The whole time we'd been waiting, my girls hadn't been able to stop chattering.

For that matter, they *never* stopped chattering, not even in their sleep, it seemed. I was used to it, but Mattias was a single man with no children. He spent his days surrounded almost exclusively by grown men, and I sincerely doubted their talk ever came close to the inanity that came out of my daughters' mouths.

By the time the hostess had seated us, the girls had already gushed over who was cuter among Austin Cooper, Blake Kozlow, and Axel Johansson (no need to add Levi into the mix, since everyone already knew he was the cutest of the cute); debated the likelihood that the four girls could end up married to the four cute hockey players; informed Mattias that they'd added Cooper, Kozlow, and Johansson to the brother-husband list ("It's like sister-wives in reverse, and they're all hockey players," Izzy explained patiently upon seeing Mattias's confused expression); and hatched a plan for the four of them to split up, travel to the various NHL cities around North America, and snatch the wayward brother-husbands who didn't play in Portland. After hearing all that, *I* was exhausted. I could only imagine that *he* was rethinking his plan to take us all to dinner and trying to come up with a good excuse to get out of it.

But he came with us, and once Sophie claimed a seat on one of the booth's benches, he inched in beside her. The other three girls gave me giggling glances and piled into the bench opposite them, leaving me to take the final spot next to Mattias. He was so large that I had to be right up against him or else I'd be practically falling out of the booth. I did my best to calm my nerves as I slid in beside him. As if it were the most natural thing in the world he could possibly do, he put his arm around my waist, his hand resting on the curve between my waist and my hip, and drew me as close to his side as I could possibly be.

His body heat was intoxicating, but nothing could have come close to his scent in terms of making me want to get even closer. He smelled like heaven, and it was all I could do to keep myself from burying my nose against his chest and sniffing my fill. It was a good thing the girls were here and we were very much in public, because otherwise I might be hard-pressed not to do my best to crawl up on his lap. That would be taking things way too far, way too fast, particularly since tonight was going to be it.

Not that I'd gotten Mattias to agree to end things after this one *date*, but he had to see the reason behind it. His sister had Down syndrome. He understood, even if he didn't want to admit it.

"Balloon!" Sophie squealed, pointing toward a man making balloon animals a few tables away from us. Then she was bouncing on the bench, unable to contain her excitement. I hid a smile, hoping she would never lose her childlike enthusiasm.

"Do you want him to make you something?" Mattias asked, chuckling.

She was too excited to do anything more than nod, and I was impressed by her restraint in staying seated where she was. Under normal circumstances, I would expect her to crawl under the table, bumping her head and knocking into legs as she went. But with Mattias beside her, she stayed relatively in place and let him wave the balloon man over.

The man smiled at Mattias and me before zeroing in on Sophie. "How about a crown for the little princess?" He was already in the process of filling a pink balloon with air.

She bounced in her seat. "Can I have a dog? I want a dog."

Pink could lead to a meltdown. I'd never figured out why, but Sophie couldn't stand the color. She didn't want it anywhere near her, typically throwing a fit of epic proportions if someone gave her a pink anything. I started to tell the balloon man that maybe pink wasn't the best color, but Mattias stopped me with a big hand enveloping mine. I shot my gaze up to meet his.

He shook his head. "Let her tell him," he mouthed at me. He didn't even know what I was about to say to the man, but he must have sensed my intent.

I bit down on my tongue. Maybe he was right. I couldn't always do everything for her. Someday, I would have to let go. She was already eleven years old, not to mention fiercely independent. She wanted to do everything she could by herself. She wanted to be as grown-up as her older sisters. She was starting to discover her wings; I needed to let her fly, even if sometimes she might fall.

The balloon man winked at her. "A dog it is, then." In no time, he was twisting the pink thing into shape.

"Not pink. No pink." Sophie's tone bordered on temper tantrum, and my blood pressure started to rise.

Mattias squeezed my hand.

"Not pink?" the balloon man repeated. In a smooth move, he shoved his half-finished project into the bag slung over his shoulder and took out a plastic bag filled with balloons of every color imaginable. "Tell me what color you want, then."

"Purple," she said emphatically, surprising the heck out of me. Purple was often her second most dreaded color. But she grinned up at Mattias and plucked at her Storm jersey. "He needs to match," she explained.

"Good call," Mattias said. "That'll make him look like he belongs with us."

With us. The way he said it made it sound like there was an *us*, Mattias included.

"Can you get me a real puppy, Bergy?" she asked, all sunshine and innocence.

"I think you'll have to ask your mom about that," he replied, cleanly deflecting her question so he wouldn't end up as either the bad guy or the hero.

"Mom?" she asked, and her sisters chimed in with promises of how they'd be the ones to feed and water and walk and wash, all of which they'd tried leveraging against me time and again.

"We'll talk about it later," I said as the waiter came over to take our orders.

The balloon man finished her dog. He stuck around until the waiter was done, so he could make her a matching purple crown even though she hadn't asked for it. They both walked away around the same time, and Sophie was grinning from ear to ear with her crown on her head and her balloon dog tucked in beside her on the bench.

"What's his name?" Mattias asked, angling his head in the balloon dog's direction.

"Levi," Sophie said emphatically.

He let out a silent chuckle, one I could feel rather than hear, and I fell for him a little harder.

THE INSTANT HE parked in my driveway, all four of my girls barreled out of his SUV and rushed straight for the door.

"Kissy-kissy time," Evie said in a sing-song voice amid their chorus of giggles, and I let out a groan.

Zoe took her keys out of her pocket and let them in, and then Mattias and I were alone for the first time. She slammed the door closed behind them. Within seconds, I saw the curtains flutter. Which meant they were peeking out at us.

"They meant to say thank you," I said on a sigh. I turned to find him staring at me with those intense blue-gray eyes. They should have frozen me, like icicles boring into me, but there was so much heat in them I burned instead. I couldn't look in those eyes very long or I'd melt into his floorboard. I hurried to speak again before I forgot how. "So thank you. For everything. This whole weekend…"

My words trailed off, along with my ability to think, because he took my hand in his again, lacing our fingers together and sending jolts of electric awareness through my veins at breakneck speed.

"I should be the one thanking you," he said. "And your girls, too."

I shook my head, unable to process it. "What? Why?"

With the pad of his thumb, he traced lazy circles on the back of my hand, raising goose bumps all up and down my arms. I shivered, but not from cold.

"Because you showed me I could be the man my sister loves even when I'm not with her."

I still didn't follow. I hadn't known Mattias very long, but he'd repeatedly shown himself to be kind, thoughtful, and entirely too much man for me to ignore. But now it was time for me to give him that kiss and get out, before I fell too hard. Before Sophie fell too hard. Before we all got too attached. It was happening, faster than I'd been prepared for, and I was already dreading the damage control I'd have to do once he walked out of our lives. I'd let him in further than anyone since Dan and I had split up under the pressure of raising a daughter with special needs. Ever since then, I'd been cautious to keep enough of a barrier between us and the rest of the world that no one could cut us too deeply, but with Mattias I'd let down my guard.

He cleared his throat before my thoughts were coherent, and I forced myself to meet his gaze again.

"I've got to head out of town in a couple of days with the team. We have a short road trip. We'll be back on Friday, though, so I was wondering—"

"I meant what I said earlier," I cut in. I tried to tug my hand away, but he tightened his hold, keeping me firmly in his grasp—exactly where my body wanted to be, and maybe my heart, too. The only part of me not on board with that was my head, which was the part I needed to be listening to. "I really appreciate everything you've done for my girls, especially for Sophie, but I think we should just end this—"

"I wondered if you had plans next weekend," he continued, as though I hadn't tried to give him a brush off. "You and the girls, I mean. Friday is Valentine's Day, so I thought—"

"The girls— It's their father's weekend with them, so it would just be me." And as soon as I said that, I realized I shouldn't have. I should have told him I had to work. Or I was going out of town. Or anything but what I'd said, really, because now he was looking at me with that panty-melting smile again, and I couldn't make myself look away. Hell, I didn't even want to. I wanted to keep staring into those eyes and feeling the jittery sensations he made me feel for as long as possible.

"So I could have you all to myself for the weekend?" Mattias said, and his smile turned into this wicked, sinful, delicious expression that made me want things I hadn't even thought about in years.

"I…"

He brushed the backs of his knuckles along my cheek, and my nipples pebbled in response. Then his lips were on mine, soft and smooth, gently coaxing me to open for him. I did, fisting my hand in his thick hair as his tongue met mine and drove me to a frenzied ache I'd thought dormant.

He hooked an arm around my waist and dragged me across the seat until I was practically in his lap. In fact, that seemed like a good idea, so I raised myself up on my knees and straddled him, steadying myself with a hand on his strong shoulder and the steering wheel pressing against the small of my back. My fingers itched to explore more of the muscles beneath them, but reason returned before I did anything stupid. My girls were watching every bit of this.

When I broke away, his breathing was as labored and ragged as mine, and he looked at me with an expression of wonder.

This had been a bad idea. A very bad idea. I should have kept it to a simple kiss, nothing more. For that matter, I should never have let it get this far. Yesterday, when we'd first encountered Mattias and Levi in the concourse, I should have wrangled my girls and gone to our regular seats. If I had, then I wouldn't be feeling so torn right now. I wouldn't be debating how I was going to come out of this with my heart intact, let alone how I would protect Sophie and my other daughters from getting too attached to this man who had his own responsibilities to worry about. I wouldn't be staring down into the eyes of a man who looked like he wanted to toss me over his shoulder and carry me back to his cave to do sweaty, dirty, amazing things to me. I wouldn't be thinking I wanted to let him.

"I should go in," I forced myself to say. I needed to get off him, but my body wouldn't cooperate, and Mattias didn't seem inclined to let me go, anyway. He had both hands on my waist, strong and steady. Big. The longer he left those hands on my body, the more I wanted to feel them.

"You probably should," he said, without even blinking.

"Yeah. I definitely should."

"All right." But he gripped my hips more tightly and drew me closer to him, until my chest was pressed up against his. He dipped his head, and I thought he was going to kiss me again. I tried to prepare myself for the sensual assault, only to have him rest his forehead against mine, both of us taking in labored breaths. "Can I pick you up when I get back into town on Friday?" His breath smelled like the spearmint mints he'd passed out to each of us as we'd left the restaurant.

I should have said no. But I didn't. I didn't even come close. "Yes," I said. Then I forced myself to climb off him, ease over to the other side of the SUV, and get out, grabbing my purse as my feet hit the concrete.

"Seems like a long time away." He winked, and my chest squeezed. "I'll give you an update on what we can do to help Sophie skate then."

I nodded, biting down on my lower lip. Then I turned and headed inside, doing my best to keep my feet moving forward. When I opened the door, I heard him back down the driveway at the same time as all four of my girls raced away from the window, giggling and leaving the curtains fluttering like my heart.

Chapter Five

Mattias

PAIGE ANSWERED THE door wearing a cream-colored dress that fit her body like a glove and made my mouth water. Her hair was swept off her neck in some sort of up-do that made it look simple but was probably really complicated and time-consuming. I didn't care about that. All I cared about was the fact that it gave me an excellent view of her long neck, and it made me want to kiss her in that spot just under her ear.

I hadn't seen her since I'd dropped her and the girls off at her house on Sunday evening, but I'd talked to her every day since. After I was done with whatever work I'd had to get done for the evening, or following the night's game when I was back in my hotel room, I'd sent her a text message to see if she was still up. Every night, she'd responded by calling me almost as soon as I'd hit send. It was as if she wanted to hear my voice as much as I needed to hear hers.

During those calls, she'd told me stories about the girls and their time at school, or bits and pieces about the clients who came to her house for massage. I'd told her about the places we stopped on the road, or the tribute the Rangers had put on for a soldier who surprised his overly pregnant wife by showing up at the arena instead of being on a video call like she'd expected. The shock had been so great that she'd gone into labor. They'd rushed the couple off to the hospital, and the baby was born before the second intermission.

Our calls had always been easy like that, a simple recounting of our days. It was as if we were old friends, like we'd known each other for years.

I'd never had that sort of relationship with any of the women I'd dated before. They'd always been so self-absorbed that all they cared about was what sorts of presents I'd bring home for them when I came back. With Paige, it was the complete opposite. I had to encourage her to tell me about herself, because she wanted to hear about me or tell me about her girls. It was as though she was lost in the mix, and I hated the thought of allowing that to continue. So I asked about her every chance I got, and she slowly started to tell me.

In all those calls, I'd never completely lost my mind and told her that I was falling for her. It seemed too soon for that, besides the fact that it wasn't the sort of thing that should be said over the phone. But everything about being with Paige felt right. It was one of those things like playing hockey, something that had come as naturally to me as breathing. I wanted to know everything there was to know about her daughters, her life, her day-to-day goings-on. I wanted to tell her everything there was to know about mine. I wanted to hear her voice and learn the sounds she made when she was surprised or overwhelmed. I wanted to ease some of her burdens. I didn't understand it, but I couldn't deny it.

And now, with her standing just inside her doorway in that dress, with her neck bare and a nervous smile lighting up her face, I couldn't seem to form a coherent thought. I held out the vase of flowers I'd brought her—yellow tulips, like Zoe had told me her mother liked—and stood there like an idiot.

With a hint of a blush, she reached for the bouquet. "Hi," she said, sounding as breathless and anxious as I felt. Because, whether the first date, when her girls came with us, could really be considered a date or not, tonight would be. I hadn't been on a date in so long I didn't know what to do with myself. It appeared I wasn't alone in that.

"Hi," I repeated.

She held up a finger, silently begging me for a moment. I nodded, and she waved me inside before setting the vase down on a cabinet just inside the door and disappearing up the stairs. I took the time while she was gone to explore. Her house wasn't simply a house; it was a home. The furniture looked cushy and comfortable. The walls were painted in warm colors and covered with family photographs and artwork surely brought home from school by the girls. The short, wide cabinet where she'd set the tulips was littered with ponytail holders, lipsticks, notes, device chargers and cords, and colored paper and markers. A row of backpacks, purses, and coats hung above it in a sort of organized chaos. It all reminded me of my parents' home, not perfectly neat and tidy but well lived-in and loved.

I was poring over a group of photos from a family vacation when Paige came back down the stairs with a piece of gray construction paper in her hands.

"From Sophie," she said, thrusting it into my hands. "She made me promise I'd give it to you when I saw you."

I glanced down and found her childlike handwriting in purple marker.

> *Dear Bergy,*
>
> *Thank you for teachen me hokey. Thank you for Levi. Thank you for diner. You are real nice. You mad me smile. You mad Mom smile. I hope you kiss Mom again. A lot. I like you. Zoe Evie and Izzy like you. Mom likes kisses.*
>
> *Love,*
> *Sophie*

She'd drawn a stick figure family of six, one much larger than the others. They all had long hair and skirts except for the big one. She'd drawn something small next to the littlest stick figure, which I assumed to be her balloon dog, Levi. Her handwriting was difficult to interpret, but I understood her meaning even if she had some problems with spelling and grammar.

"She's already attached," Paige said when I looked up. She had tears in her eyes, which I brushed away with my thumb. She shook her head and stepped away, not allowing me to comfort her. "I worried this would happen."

"Is that so horrible? I'm not going to hurt her, Paige." That was the last thing I would ever want to do.

"You won't mean to." She shrugged and gave me the most pathetic look imaginable. "Why couldn't you have been mean and horrible? All of this would have been so much easier if you were awful, you know."

I laughed. "Depending on who you ask, they'll tell you all about how mean and horrible I am. Burnzie might have a few choice words to say after the way I laid into him last night, for one, and I lost track of how many guys have called me the meanest son of a bitch they ever played against a while back."

She shook her head. "But that's… That's not you. It's not the real you."

I wasn't sure who the *real* me was. It probably depended on whom I was with. There was the version that Linnea saw…the one that came out when I was with Paige and her girls. And then there was the other version, the one that everyone else saw.

Arguing about it wasn't going to change anything, though. I held out a hand for her. "Come on. Let's go have some fun and worry about all of this later." Not that I expected her to ever stop worrying. It went with the territory when you had a daughter with Down syndrome. Still, she had the whole weekend free from her kids, and I intended to make good use of that time in getting to know *Paige*.

She picked up her purse and put her hand in mine. "Fine. No worrying, at least for now."

Little did she know, I intended the *for now* part to last the entire weekend.

MATTIAS TOOK ME to dinner at El Gaucho for our Valentine's Day date, an upscale steak restaurant downtown that I would never consider going to under normal circumstances. Granted, *normal circumstances* meant having all of my girls with me, since Dan only kept them one weekend a month, on average. He was supposed to have them every other weekend, but his job prevented that from happening. With tax season coming up, he might not be able to keep them at all after this weekend for at least the next couple of months, so I was determined to enjoy this one with Mattias, whether my girls were with us or not.

Fun, bright places were always better when they were along—Sophie, in particular—and El Gaucho was dimly lit, elegant, and exceedingly romantic.

It was easy to fall right back into the trap of falling for Mattias in that sort of setting. There were candles and more flowers on our table, and he kept leaning in closer to me, resting his chin on his hand and staring so deep into my eyes it felt as though he could see all the way down to my soul.

A Latin band was playing off in the distance, and our waiter flambéed parts of our meal directly beside our table. I oohed and aahed more than I expected I would, but how often could I experience something like this? Not very. As a single mom, I had more academic meets, soccer games, and laundry days on my calendar than dates. But I couldn't imagine anywhere I'd rather be or anyone I'd rather be with.

Once the waiter left us with our meal, Mattias leaned in again, thoroughly invested in me in a way that made me feel heady. "You've never told me how you got into massage. Did you always want to do it?"

I shook my head, sipping from the robust red wine he'd ordered for us. "Not always, no. I came to it in a roundabout way."

He raised a brow, a silent encouragement for me to continue.

"I was in college when I met Dan. We were both accounting students. We got married when he graduated, in the summer after my sophomore year. I was pregnant with Zoe before Christmas break in my senior year, and I never ended up finishing my degree. We decided it would be better for us both if I was a stay-at-home mom, at least while the girls were little. By then, he was getting ready for his CPA exam, and he was already making a decent living. But then Sophie came along, and she needed a lot of extra care—like daily massage. When she was a baby, her therapist taught me to massage her little body, to help with her blood flow and to increase her muscle tone and awareness. It was a sensory thing, too—a way for me and Sophie to connect. It was something I did for her three times a day, every day, for the first few years of her life. By the time she was three, Dan and I were both so stressed with all of her appointments and visits and therapy sessions that we just…fell apart. We didn't know each other anymore. There was no time for us to be a couple. The stress of it all drove this huge chasm between us, and we were never able to recover from it. But when we divorced, I knew I needed a job of some sort. Preferably something where I could set my own hours and work either at home or close to home, and massage seemed like a good fit. I started my training as soon as Dan moved out of the house, and the rest is history."

Mattias hadn't looked away the whole time I spoke. He had been eating some, but honestly he'd paid far more attention to me than he had to his meal. It was a very rare thing for me to have someone's undivided attention. I was far more used to having my own attention split multiple ways, trying to make sure each of my daughters had everything they needed and none of them felt neglected.

He reached across the table and let his fingertips fall on the back of my hand, sending electric jolts up my arm. I bit down on my lip, and he grinned, like he knew he was the cause of my nerves. "No regrets?" he asked. "You don't wish you'd gone back to college to finish your degree? I can tell from the way you talk about your job now that you love it, but…"

"No regrets. I don't believe in them. And I do love my job. Actually, I'll be taking some continuing ed courses next month that you might be interested in. I already do deep tissue work, trigger point, that sort of thing, but I'm going to learn about sports massage."

He made an appreciative humming sound and raised a brow. "If you ever need a guinea pig to practice on, I'm sure it wouldn't take much arm twisting to get some of the boys on board."

"I'll keep that in mind," I said, winking at him.

In truth, I was slightly shocked and more than just a bit disappointed that he hadn't volunteered himself. I'd been dying to get my hands on him—*really* explore his muscles—ever since I'd first seen him last weekend. Having watched his players and spent some time close to Mattias, he seemed as fit as any of them, and likely a heck of a lot stronger than many of them. There was a certain sort of strength that came to men as they got older, and I had no doubt he had it in spades.

I speared a piece of roasted potato with my fork and popped it into my mouth. Then I almost melted from how good it was. "How do they make something so simple taste *so good*?" I asked, still chewing.

"Something tells me they won't be giving us their secrets."

"Too bad. I could teach the girls to make it, and then we could make a killing out of my kitchen."

"I doubt the government would look too kindly on slave labor," he joked.

"No slaves involved. We'd call it their chores and pay them an allowance. It'd be all aboveboard."

He laughed. Mattias had a rich, deep laugh, much like his voice. It rumbled through me and made me want to be closer to him, to feel it beneath my touch. Once I started thinking along those lines, though, I doubted I'd be able to stop anytime soon. I bit my lower lip again.

"If you don't stop doing that, I'm going to have to join you," he said.

I arched a brow in question.

"Biting your lip."

"Be careful not to hurt yourself."

He lifted his wineglass and tilted it in my direction. "I meant I'd bite your lip."

I downed a large swallow from my own glass to hide the rush of heat that flooded my face, not that it was likely to do any good. Besides, I wasn't fifteen. I was a grown woman. I could flirt and tease and talk about adult things without blushing like my daughters would, couldn't I? Determined to prove I could, even if only to myself, I met his gaze. "Try not to draw blood when you do."

"Is that an invitation?"

"More like a promise of things to come."

He sipped and let the wine roll over his tongue for a moment before swallowing, taking his time to answer. "I like promises," he finally said. "Maybe as much as you like kisses."

So apparently keeping myself from blushing was going to be next to impossible. As soon as I'd seen what Sophie had written in her letter to him, I'd known he was going to pounce all over that one. Good to see he didn't intend to let me down on that score.

I cut into my steak, searching my brain for any topic I could turn to in order to deflect the attention away from me, at least for long enough that I could refocus my thoughts. With Sophie on my mind, the first safe subject that came to me was Mattias's sister.

"So, does your sister ever come to visit you?" I asked, taking a large bite of steak so I wouldn't have to talk too soon.

A soft expression came into his eyes the second I mentioned his sister, but he shook his head. "Not often. Linnea lives in a group home in Stockholm, and our parents are close by. I spend as much time with her as I can when I'm home in the summers, but it never feels like enough." He stopped there and shook his head, as if he didn't want to go on.

"What?" I asked.

He shrugged. "I told you she has a boyfriend and she wants to live with him now, didn't I?" When I nodded, he said, "His name's Johan. He was the one who helped hold her together when her first boyfriend died about five years ago. I was here, coaching. I couldn't be there to help out, and my parents were at a loss about how to help her understand and grieve. But Johan took Linnea under his wing. He brought a book to work one day. *Adjö, herr Muffin*, it was called. *Good-bye, Mr. Muffin*. It's meant to help kids understand about death and grief. He took her aside on their break and read it to her, and he let her cry on his shoulder. That started a routine. Every day, he would bring some children's book or another to read to her. They had been coworkers for a long time, and they'd been friendly before that, but they started getting a lot closer because he brought his books to read and share with her."

"And then he took her out for ice cream," I said, smiling as his voice trailed off.

"And then he took her out for ice cream," Mattias repeated, nodding with a sheepish chuckle. "And now she wants to live with him."

"Sounds like he's a good guy." Maybe a lot like the man sitting next to me and staring at me like he never wanted to look anywhere else. My belly flipped at the unwavering look in his eyes.

"He is. He's a very good man."

"Does it ease your mind at all to know that?" I asked. "I mean, she could have fallen for someone who would have been the worst sort of influence on her, and then what?"

"Is your mind ever going to be at ease when it comes to your girls?"

"Good point. As boy crazy as they are..."

"But they know a good man when they see one," Mattias said emphatically. Like he knew them well enough to know that.

I shook my head, my brows pinching together.

"501's a good man," he explained. "Way too old for them, but he's a good man. I think they can sense it. They've got good instincts when it comes to their hormonal crushes." He reached across the table. I thought he was going for the saltshaker, but he took my hand instead, and he winked. "Like their mom."

My earlier belly flips couldn't hold a candle to what was going on internally now. I was seriously melting. So were my panties. They were all, *poof*, gone. Just like that.

Or they would be if we weren't sitting in the middle of a crowded restaurant.

Chapter Six

Paige

AFTER A DINNER filled with the most intoxicating mix of heady flirtation, banter, and soul-baring conversation, Mattias took me to a play at Portland Center Stage. It was over, and we were on our way back to my house, but I honestly didn't know if the play had been any good or not. The whole time we'd been there, I'd been so caught up in the sensation of Mattias's arm draped casually over my shoulders and the heat of his body warming me down to my toes that I couldn't pay attention to anything happening up on stage.

In fact, even now as we made our way through Portland's neighborhoods, I couldn't make my brain cooperate. No matter how hard I tried to think like a rational adult, my recently acquired reverse-aging process was raging, and my hormones were in complete control. All I wanted to do was take him inside my house the second we got there and jump him. I couldn't even remember the last time I'd been this out of control with lustful urges. Years. Maybe more than a decade.

I couldn't do a damn thing about it while he was still driving, though.

My cell phone beeped with a text message. Probably Zoe. She was always good about checking in with me when the girls were with their father or otherwise not with me. I assumed it had something to do with her being the eldest.

I dug around in my purse for my phone. It beeped again, and then a couple more times before I finally pulled it free. As soon as I wrapped my fingers around it, I unlocked the screen as I drew it out.

Then I burst out snort-laughing at Zoe's series of messages.

> *Are you having a good time with Beefy? Getting kissy-faced yet? You should totally take him inside and make out with him on the couch like you're a teenager. We promise we won't walk in on you and ruin the fun, like you would do to us. We're cooler than that.*

> *OMG. Beefy! Beefy. BEEFY.*

> *Stupid phone.*

> *B E R G Y. I meant Beefy.*

> *Gah! Autocorrect is killing me.*

> *Just make out with him, 'kay? You deserve a good make-out session. And pretend you never saw this. I'm going to go crawl under a rock and die now.*

Mattias angled his head toward me, attempting to hold back a laugh of his own. "That good? Do I want to know?"

I shook my head and tried to stop laughing, but it was no use. *Beefy*. Every time I read it, my mind changed it to *Beefcake*, which was way too appropriate. Not to mention inappropriate. That wasn't something anyone needed to know other than me, not even my girls. If I let it slip to one of them? They'd be chanting it every chance they got, and he would be bound to find out at some point. No chance I wanted him to see it because then I'd have to find a way to explain without putting my foot in my mouth, and that didn't seem even remotely likely.

"If it's that funny, I need to know. Fair's fair."

"Just a text from Zoe," I forced out between snorts and guffaws.

"Mm-hmm. *Just* a text. Your phone went off at least five times, and now you're laughing so hard you can hardly breathe."

I needed to deflect him, and fast since he wasn't giving up. "Autocorrect issues."

"Those are the best. Now you *have* to tell me." He smiled, and my pulse kicked up a notch or two.

"Just something that happened to her today at school," I hedged, angling myself so he couldn't accidentally read what was on my screen.

He came to a red light and stopped the car, turning more fully to face me. Based on experience, the light at this intersection would be a long one, too. Crap.

"If it's something from school, why are *you* blushing so hard?"

"I'm probably purple from laughing until I was out

of breath."

He narrowed his eyes. "I think it's about me."

"It's not about you," I lied, even though I knew I was a horrible liar. Always had been. I should have taken acting classes in school or something. Anything to help me put on a mask and convince him I was telling the truth.

Not that I wanted to make a habit of lying, but it would be a good skill to have on occasion.

"So it is about me, then." He grinned, that sexy, panty-melting one again. It made me want to crawl back into his lap, and I didn't want to stop with just a kiss this time. He looked like he knew exactly what I was thinking. In fact, he looked like he would be completely on board with doing exactly that if we weren't sitting in the middle of an intersection. "I swear, I won't let on that I know, whatever it is. I won't ask you to take a screenshot so we can post it all over the Internet. I wouldn't embarrass you or your girls like that…"

"She would *die* if I let you see it. And then she'd murder me."

"If she was already dead, she couldn't do anything to you," he pointed out, invoking reason—something that had escaped me the second he'd walked into my life.

"Then her sisters would kill me."

He shook his head, clearly fighting back another laugh. "What did she say? You can't keep it from me."

I was reaching for my purse to hide the evidence when he made a grab for my phone. He was lightning fast, snatching it out of my grip before I could rip it away from him.

"Beefy? That's…"

"Awful," I finished for him.

"I was thinking more along the lines of hilarious, but

we can go with awful if you want."

I pressed my eyes closed, sinking down in my seat. "If she finds out you've seen this…"

"Our secret." He tossed the phone back to me just as the light changed.

I punched in a quick response for her and hit Send before shoving the phone back in my purse.

"So what did you tell her about the whole getting kissy-faced on the sofa idea?" he asked, not even attempting to make the question casual. His words were heated. Needy. Somehow, there was still a hint of humor in it but not enough to outweigh the sensual quality it had taken on. The deep tone of his voice rumbled through my body, jump-starting my sex drive like nobody's business.

I couldn't seem to catch my breath. For once in my life, I didn't mind that I couldn't. I nibbled on my lower lip. "I told her she needed to worry about herself and her sisters and leave me alone."

"You and Beefy, you mean. To leave us alone."

In my mind, I turned it to *Beefcake* again. I let out a nervous laugh and bit my tongue to keep from saying it aloud. "Yes, me and Beefy."

He turned onto my street and rolled into the driveway, but he didn't turn off the engine. He put the car in park and turned in his seat to face me, that same panty-melting smile on his face, and he trailed the tips of his fingers up the back of my hand. Every touch, no matter how seemingly insignificant or barely there, had my body buzzing like an agitated beehive.

"I'm not going to lie," he said after a long minute. "I want you to ask me to come in. I like the idea of testing out Zoe's suggestion. I think she's onto something, and I think we should explore it. But if you aren't on board with that or if you think we'd be rushing things, I'll walk you to your door and then go."

"Without even a good-night kiss?"

He winked. "I would hope you'd allow me that, at the very least, but I'd understand if you didn't want it."

I wasn't inclined to let things stop with a simple good-night kiss. I mean, how often would a chance like this present itself? I was almost forty, and most of my evenings were claimed by my daughters. They would be for a long time to come, too, even though they were growing up far faster than I would like sometimes. I probably wouldn't have another kid-free night for at least a couple of months. It had been an eternity since I'd been with a man, and there was no telling how long it might be until the next opportunity presented itself.

I screwed up my courage and decided to go for it. "I'm not sure I'll be satisfied with just a kiss."

"No?"

"No. Why don't you shut off the ignition and come in with me?"

"Oh, thank God."

Mattias

WE BARELY HAD the front door closed when Paige was practically climbing me, like she was trying to crawl inside my body. And damn if I didn't want to let her. We both removed our coats, tossing them on the hall cabinet along with her purse to join the array I'd discovered earlier.

I leaned back against the door and dragged her forward by her hips until she was nestled right up against me. I couldn't get enough of her curves. Every time she'd allowed me to guide her with a hand on her back, I'd been dying to really touch her, to explore her body.

Paige was petite and fit. Some women who worked hard to stay in shape lost most of their curves, toning until they were almost as straight and angular as me. Not Paige. She had the sexiest ass, one that her dress hugged and accented in a way that made my mouth water. I slipped my hands down and back, exploring how tight it was, its perfect shape, and she burrowed closer to me. My cock came to attention then, more urgently than it had been to that point, pressing into her belly. We fit together seamlessly, soft against hard, her curves molding to me in an addictive way. It was like we were made for each other.

"I want to feel your hands on me," she said, breathless, tugging my shirt up from my pants. "Everywhere. On my skin. And I want to touch you. I want to learn everything there is to know about your body, to memorize the feel of you."

When she freed my hem, I still hadn't processed the fact that the very thing I'd been unable to stop thinking about for the last week was really happening. Her fingertips teased my abs as she slid them up my torso.

"Weren't we supposed to be taking this to the couch?" I asked.

She popped open a couple of my buttons. "We could take it straight to the bedroom."

I fought down a groan. "No point wasting time?"

In lieu of an answer, she took my hand and took charge, leading me up the stairs and down the hall. She didn't leave me any time to take in my surroundings. She spun me around and pushed on my chest with both hands, and I fell back onto the bed. I reached for her as I collapsed, gripping her thighs and drawing her up so she straddled me. That forced her dress to inch upward. Starting at the backs of her knees, I teased her sensitive skin as I began my study of her—learning what she liked; discovering her erogenous zones; discerning if she preferred soft or hard, fast or slow, rough or gentle.

As I trailed my fingers up the backs of her thighs, my eyes never leaving hers, she made short work of undoing my shirt and pushing it back over my shoulders. She raked her eyes over my chest, and then she followed the same path with her hands.

When Paige touched me, it was unlike any other woman's touch I'd ever experienced. It was as if her hands were an extension of her soul, and she was using them to find mine. I'd had plenty of massages in my day, but this was as different as night and day. She followed a path her hands knew well, even though she'd never had those hands on me before, exploring the way the various muscles came together.

Then she dropped her head and used her tongue to follow the same trail her fingers had just blazed. I sucked in a sharp breath.

Paige lifted her head enough that she could look in my eyes, her tongue on my skin. I propped myself up on my elbows so I could watch, content for now to let her do as she would.

She traced the lines of my pecs with her tongue, lazily moving closer to my nipple and driving me out of my mind with need. When she reached it, she flicked her tongue a couple of times before taking it into her mouth and sucking, and my cock jerked as if *that* was where she had her mouth. With a lusty laugh, she wiggled her hips.

That was enough to brush the heat of her center over the tip of my cock. Never mind the fact that we were both almost fully clothed. I was practically desperate to get inside her, but at the same time, I hated the thought of putting an end to her ministrations. Paige Calhoun was a woman who knew what she wanted, and I'd be damned if I didn't let her have it.

She inched upward, focusing her attention on the hollow at the base of my neck.

"You're killing me," I ground out.

"You want me to stop?"

Hell no. But I wanted to give as good as I got. "Tell me what you want. Show me what you like."

"I want you. Naked. And I want to get my hands on every hard inch of your body."

"I think we can make that happen." I put a hand on the small of her back to support her as I flipped our positions, momentarily crushing her to the mattress.

She let out a sharp gasp, but a needy moan soon followed. I kissed her chin and straightened away from her so I could get up and strip. With her eyes taking in my every move, devouring me as I bared myself to her, she bit down on her lower lip. She was so fucking sexy when she did that. It made me think about her using those teeth to nip my flesh. With those thoughts racing through my head, I couldn't get my clothes off fast enough.

I tossed them all in a heap on the floor and crawled back into the bed, supporting myself above her with my arms. She still had every stitch of her clothes on, right down to the slinky heels she'd worn tonight. My hands were itching to peel that dress off her body, but I was just as anxious to see what she would do next.

Starting at my wrists, she slid her hands up my arms,

a painstaking inch at a time. Good thing I still worked out as much as I had in my playing days, because she wasn't in any rush to move on to the next bit. When she got to my shoulders, she put one hand on the back of my neck and drew me down to kiss her.

As soon as our lips touched, her mouth was open and waiting. I slid my tongue inside to meet hers, and they tangled together the way we'd done that first time, both languid and urgent at once.

She didn't stop there, gliding her hands down the expanse of my back and opening her legs so I could settle between them. If not for her dress and panties, I could already be where I wanted to be—so deep inside her that her toes would curl. I groaned against her mouth when she reached my ass and gripped each cheek like she meant it, drawing me closer still to her heat. When she rolled her hips, I nearly lost it.

I broke off the kiss and ground out, "I need to be inside you." It had been too damn long since I'd been with a woman. I didn't know how much longer I could hold out, especially with the sensual torment she was putting me through.

She gave me a sultry, slinky grin. "Roll over."

It was about time. I did what she told me to, bringing her with me and trying to figure out how to get her dress off her as soon as she was no longer trapped beneath my weight. I tugged at the hem, attempting to peel it up and over her head, but that didn't work very well. It only moved a bit.

She shook her head, though, and slipped out of my grasp.

I was a patient man, normally, but Paige was seriously trying it right now.

Kneeling on the edge of the bed, she resumed her

careful survey of my body by inching her way up my legs. By the time she reached my knees, I broke out in a sweat, desperate for more. When she lowered her head and licked the inside of my thigh, it was all I could do to fist my hands in her bedding instead of her hair.

She worked her way higher slowly. Meticulously. A brief touch of her tongue to the vee line of my oblique muscles. Then I couldn't help it. My hips bucked up, an involuntary reaction to her being so close to where I wanted her. I could feel her smile against my skin. She settled herself between my thighs. Lowered her head. Took me in her mouth.

I was in heaven.

Paige

MATTIAS KEPT FISTING and releasing the comforter. I thought about telling him he could grab hold of my hair and direct me where he wanted me, but that would require taking a break from what I was doing.

He was reveling in it too much for me to stop my efforts now. His enjoyment gave me supreme satisfaction, so I focused on giving him the best blow job of his life. It was one thing that, in all the years I'd been married, Dan had never gotten bored with. I knew how to suck a man off. Until I'd gotten Mattias down on the bed and put my hands on him, I hadn't realized just how much I'd missed it. I got my hands in on the act, gently massaging his balls with one as I used the other to assist me in covering more ground.

I dipped down again, and he brought his knees up on either side of me, straining with the effort to let me pleasure him without grinding his hips up into me.

"*Ja*," he said, his voice rough and husky, cracking from exertion even though I was the one currently doing all the work. He'd have his turn soon enough. "*Det är så bra, sötnos.*"

The fact that he was speaking in Swedish only reconfirmed the idea that I was rocking his world, even though I didn't have the first clue what he meant. I ramped up my efforts, swirling my tongue around his head before taking him in as deeply as I could manage.

Then he did put a hand on the back of my head, gently urging me to bob. If that was what he wanted, that was what I'd give him. Relaxing so he could take control of things, I allowed myself to exult in the sensation of his hot, hard erection filling me in this way.

"Paige," he said, easing me up and off his length.

I shot my eyes up to meet his.

He caressed my face, his thumb gliding over my cheekbone. "I can't wait anymore. I need to be inside you." He'd already said that to me before, but this time there was a sense of urgency to his words that I knew better than to ignore.

I fished through my nightstand drawer for a condom. I'd bought some while the girls were in school one day, on the off chance I'd have the opportunity to make use of them—better safe than sorry—and squashed them between the pages of an anatomy book, in case one of the girls went searching through my things for tweezers or a particular shade of fingernail polish. It took me a minute to get my hand on the little foil wrapper, but as soon as I did, I tossed it Mattias's way.

While he opened it and prepared himself, I reached over my shoulders and unclasped my dress, then eased the zipper down. Once it was loose, I allowed it to slide off my shoulders and drop down my arms, pooling at my feet. Mattias's eyes never left me. He rolled to his side and propped himself up on one elbow. When I stretched my arms behind my back to unhook my bra, he reached for himself and stroked. My breasts jiggled when the bra fell away. I fixed my thumbs in the waistband of my panties and started lowering them.

"Wait," Mattias said harshly.

I froze. "What?" Had I done something wrong? Or maybe he'd changed his mind now that he'd seen me mostly naked. Talk about making a woman self-conscious. "What's wrong?" I asked, since he didn't immediately answer.

"Sorry. Nothing's wrong." He pumped himself a few more times. "I just…I just wondered. Are you ready? Wet? You've been taking care of me, but I've hardly touched you at all."

Wet didn't even begin to cover it. As long as he wasn't having second thoughts, I decided to finish lowering my panties. Once they hit my ankles, I stepped out and toed them aside before crossing back to him.

"I'm more than ready," I said as I sat on the edge of the bed again. "But I won't try to stop you from touching me in any way you want to."

He reached for me as soon as I was close enough, tugging me down beside him. Leaning over me, he traced a finger from my collarbone to my hip, letting it whisper over my flesh. My already taut nipple juddered as he tweaked it on his meandering journey south. However much I wanted him inside me, I couldn't complain. Turnabout was only fair, and I had taken my time and then some in teasing him to a frenzy.

I brought my knee up in invitation and anticipation,

dropping my head back onto my pillow. Gradually, he edged his exploration down, lower, lower, closer to where I wanted him to be. Mattias touched the inside of my thigh and pressed it toward the bed, opening me for him to discover what he would.

With only the tip of a single finger, he outlined my lower lips. "Very wet," he murmured.

"I told you." My entire body was trembling, not from cold but from need.

One finger slipped inside me, then another, and I arched my back in bliss.

"I can't wait much longer," he said.

"I can't, either."

He pumped his fingers inside me a few times, my hips rising to meet him of their own volition. The heel of his palm brushed against my clit, and I let out a moan.

"Yes, *sötnos*," he said. "You're going to come for me, Paige. But I want it to be while I'm inside you."

I wanted that, too. More than I could say. I nodded, moaning as he removed his fingers from my channel and repositioned himself. Mattias raised himself over me again, placing his cock at my entrance. He rocked his hips a few times, only sliding an inch or two inside me at first. But then I wrapped my legs around his waist and put my hands on his shoulders, and he drove all the way home, nearly splitting me in two.

I bit down on my lower lip to keep from crying out, but I couldn't stop myself from tensing at the sting of his entrance.

"Am I hurting you?"

I shook my head, trying to buy myself another moment before answering. "It's just been so long," I finally forced out. "Give me a minute and I'll be fine."

He held himself still, resting his forehead against mine, and kissed me tenderly. "I don't want you just be fine."

The sting eased to a dull ache as my sex stretched to accommodate him. I rolled my hips to let him know I was ready. He groaned, but then he started to move within me, gentle thrusts at first that gradually increased in speed and intensity. He lifted his weight off me, staring down into my eyes as we moved together, a slick glide that felt as natural as breathing and as exhilarating as skydiving.

My body tensed as I approached orgasm. I slipped a hand between our bodies to rub my clitoris. A few more thrusts and I splintered, shuddering and burying my head in Mattias's shoulder.

He shifted our positions, lifting my legs and spreading them wider, which somehow allowed him to drive even deeper into me. Then he collapsed against me, his cock jerking inside me as he came. "*Det känns som om jag är hemma, sötnos,*" he said next to my ear.

We lay there with our limbs tangled, too done in to move despite our sweaty bodies starting to stick to one another, until our breathing returned to normal and our pulses slowed to a mere gallop. I relished the weight of him pushing me down into the mattress, the heady scent of his cologne mixing with the musk of our efforts.

I didn't want it to end.

And it wasn't just because I didn't know when the next time I would have an opportunity like this might be. I had to be honest with myself. Yes, I'd asked Mattias to come in, and I'd decided to take him to my bed *initially* because I'd wanted to indulge myself. But that was far from the whole truth of what was behind it.

I was falling for Mattias—hard—and even though I still had a thousand reasons not to humor the selfish idea of getting into a relationship, it appeared to be too late for that. Now I just had to figure out what to do about it.

He rolled off me after a long while, and I immediately felt the loss of him. I turned on my side, following him so I could rest my head on his shoulder. He trailed his fingers through my hair, an action that felt both familiar and right.

"Mattias?" I asked after a few moments.

"Hmm?"

"Tell me what you said."

He looked down at me with a question in his eyes.

"The Swedish a minute ago."

He thought for a moment. But then he said, "It was just heat-of-the-moment nonsense. Something like *I feel like I'm home, sweetie.*"

Something warm and pure bubbled up in my heart. "I don't think that's nonsense at all."

Chapter Seven

MY INTENTION WASN'T to spend the night—I would never have been so presumptuous—so I hadn't come prepared for that. After Paige and I got up, showered, dressed, and had breakfast, I had to go back to my place for clean clothes and the like before practice. I promised her that as soon as I could, I'd be back to pick her up and we could continue with our weekend together.

When I left—following a few lingering kisses—I told her to rest up and dress comfortably. The comfortable part of that was an absolute necessity because of what I had planned. We were going hiking in the Columbia River Gorge. I'd been out to Multnomah Falls a few times since I'd been in Portland, and they seemed like the perfect place for an active date. Lucky for me, the weather had cooperated today. It was cool but not too cold, considering it was February, and the sun was shining.

It was 501's first full-contact practice with the team

following his concussion, and I pushed him hard. I *always* pushed 501 hard, actually. He reminded me a lot of myself when I'd been his age. He had all the potential to be one of the best defensemen in the world, but he was still making a lot of rookie mistakes, even though it was his second year in the league. He seemed to go back and forth between sitting back and trying too hard, though, so he wasn't getting the kind of ice time he and I both knew he was capable of handling. I'd already decided that for the rest of this season and likely all of the next, he was going to be my special project. I was determined to get every ounce of effort I could squeeze out of him. He might not like it while it was going on, but he would thank me for it down the road. After practice was over, I sent him off to see Doc for another evaluation before he was cleared to play in our next game.

Then, for the first time in my career as a coach, I took off early. Webs and Handy were perfectly capable of handling all the game prep that needed to be done. Jim was always telling me I needed to take some time for myself so I wouldn't burn out, and I never took him up on it. Today? I planned to take full advantage of that.

When Paige answered the door, she was blushing and shoving her phone into the pocket of her jeans.

"Zoe checking up on you and Beefy?" I asked.

"You think I'd tell you that?" She winked, grabbed a rain jacket and her purse, and locked the door.

We spent the drive talking about my plans for helping Sophie learn to skate. Drywall had already drawn up a blueprint of sorts for the first rig he intended to build, and now that we were due to be home for a long stretch, he thought he could get at least an initial attempt put together within the next week or so.

There weren't too many cars in the parking lot when we reached the lodge at Multnomah Falls, which meant we shouldn't be overrun on our hike.

"Ready?" I asked as we climbed out of my SUV.

Paige slung the strap of her purse across her body and reached for my hand with a smile filled with trepidation. "So I guess I never mentioned my fear of heights, did I?"

I shook my head, lacing my fingers with hers. "I'll keep you safe."

Her fear didn't stop her from hiking up the trail with me. We completely bypassed the primary viewing area. That was where most of the small crowd would be, so getting out on the hiking paths would give us more privacy.

When we reached the Benson Bridge, I slowed down, not wanting to assume anything. "You up for it?" The bridge spanned the space between two halves of a ridge and looked down over the lower cascade.

She gripped my hand tighter but nodded.

We made our way to the center of the footbridge and stopped, turning toward the gushing water. A chilly spray hit our faces, and Paige nestled herself in front of me, taking both my arms and wrapping them around her waist. She was shaking, but I wasn't sure if it was fear or cold behind it.

"You're not scared?"

"I'm fine as long as I only look up, not down."

"Do your girls know you're scared of heights?" I asked.

"They know. It's too hard to hide it when they want to go on roller coasters and sky trams and God only knows what else."

"So what would they think if they could see you now?"

She waited a moment but then laughed. "They'd think you'd brainwashed me."

I took my cell phone out of my pocket and nudged her to turn so we were facing the other direction. "I think we need to send them a selfie so they can see you facing your fears."

"Oh, please don't make me look that way," she said, stiffening.

"Look up, not down. I've got you." I tightened my other arm around her, drawing her closer to me.

She waited a beat, but then she nodded resolutely.

I got us in position and held my phone out so it would catch us, the falls in the background, and at least a bit of the bridge. "Are you smiling?"

"I'm squeezing my eyes closed."

I laughed. "That's not what you want them to see, is it?"

"Maybe not, but it's as good as I can do."

There was something else she could do that I was sure would work much better. I put a finger under her chin and tilted her head up toward me, and I kissed her. When I broke it off, she said, "Oh," and blinked up at me a few times. That was when I snapped the shot.

"Give me Zoe's phone number, and I'll let her see how kissy-faced you're getting with Beefy."

"Only if you swear not to mention Beefy at all."

I pecked her on the lips again. "Done." Right now, I would promise her almost anything. I put the number in as she rattled off the digits and hit Send.

"There aren't many people in the world I'd do that for, you know," Paige said.

I spun her around in my arms so I could see her eyes. "Do what?"

"Get up here. Face my fears. You bring things out of me that I didn't know were there."

She and her girls did the same for me. Well, not exactly. I knew this side of me existed, thanks to Linnea. But until Paige and her family had come into my life, no one but Linnea could bring out that side of me, and I'd been happy to keep it that way.

I kissed her on the forehead and took her hand. "Should we keep going up, or are you ready to go down?"

"Up," she said at the same moment as my phone dinged with a reply.

Mom and Beefy, sitting in a tree. K I S S I N G.

And then my phone went crazy with more replies.

OMG. Beefy.

No. B E R G Y. Not Beefy.

I am so sorry.

I hate my phone. Stupid autocorrect.

I'm going to go crawl under a rock now. Please forget I ever existed. Tell Mom I love her.

I burst out laughing so hard and so loud it echoed through the valley.

Paige

MATTIAS SPENT THE night at my house again. We hadn't exactly had a huge conversation about it or anything. It felt right, so we let it happen.

I was already getting used to waking up in his arms, and it had only been two nights. This could only spell trouble for me, but I didn't know how to stop it. For that matter, I wasn't sure I needed to stop it anymore. He cared about my girls—enough that he was going to all sorts of trouble to keep a promise to Sophie—and they seemed to like him. This weekend, we were doing things with just the two of us, but all of our plans for the future were things that would include my daughters, and he was the one making the suggestions.

He wasn't asking me for things I wouldn't be able to give him. He didn't expect me to drop everything and be with him, and he wouldn't drop everything to be with me, either. We both had our own lives, but that didn't mean we couldn't find a way to share parts of them with each other. Did it?

Oh, and then there was the small matter that—despite the fact that we'd now had sex several times—he could still make my panties melt with nothing more than a grin. If anything, that had only increased.

I was a mess over him, but for some odd reason, I couldn't seem to make myself mind.

While he was gone to deal with practice and other work with the Storm on Sunday, I used that time to clean my house, try to make a dent in the massive piles of laundry that had built up over the course of the week, and go grocery shopping in preparation for the week to come. There was a brief moment when I debated taking a nap, but I brushed that aside. I could nap when my girls were grown and living on their own. I didn't often have time to myself like this, and I knew better than to let it go to waste.

There was still a Mt. Everest-sized pile of laundry waiting to be washed when the doorbell rang, signaling that my time alone was at an end. The instant I opened it, Mattias put his arms around me and gave me a toe-curling kiss, as if he hadn't seen me in months instead of hours. I wouldn't have minded continuing with what he'd started if not for the fact that Dan's weekend with the girls was at an end, and I needed to go pick them up.

Mattias came with me to get them. "I'll stay in the car if you think it would be better," he suggested once he'd parked in Dan's driveway.

I shook my head. "No need for that." In fact, it was better for my ex to meet Mattias now, because I had made up my mind that I wanted to take things further. I wasn't sure what it would look like, and I was even less positive what the girls were ready for, but I wanted to make things as smooth as possible for my kids. That meant their father needed to know there was a new man in my life.

Zoe answered the door and let us in, giving Mattias a wide-eyed look. "Just so you know, that was all my phone's fault."

She'd barely gotten that out before Sophie came running, arms wide for a hug. But instead of jumping into my arms, she made a flying leap for Mattias. She hugged him hard, nearly strangling him with her grip around his neck.

It was too much for me. I stepped back, blinking

down the tears stinging behind my eyes. My baby girl had decided he should be part of her life, so who was I to say otherwise? Even if I hadn't already been leaning toward making this relationship with Mattias more official, I would have given in upon seeing this.

Once Mattias extricated himself from Sophie's exuberant display of affection, he shook Dan's hand and exchanged a few pleasantries while I helped the older girls pack up the last of their things so we could head home.

We were in the SUV heading back to my place when Sophie piped up with, "Bergy?"

"Yes, Sophie?" He glanced at her in his rearview mirror.

"Good job on kissing Mom. Zoe showed me the picture."

Everyone burst out laughing, including Mattias. Everyone but me. I bit down on my lower lip, unable to decide between snort-laughing along with the rest of them or burying my head in the sand like Zoe kept threatening to do.

"Well, we had a deal, right?" he said after the laughter died down.

"Right. So when can I skate?"

He turned onto my street, smiling like he'd just won the lottery. I wasn't sure what to make of that, but he answered her before I got the chance to overanalyze it. "Soon," he said. "But first, we need to start doing some exercise so we can build up your muscles."

"Like what kind of exercise?"

"Do you know what crunches are?" he asked.

"Yep."

"Well, we'll do things like that. You'll need strong core muscles to be able to skate."

"We can all do it together," Izzy said. "So we can all skate."

"Sure," he replied, and his grin just kept getting bigger. "We can call it Workouts with Bergy or something like that."

"Can we work out with Levi?" Evie asked.

Mattias chuckled. "Not sure I can make that one happen, but maybe we can get some of the guys involved when we're ready to skate."

That was apparently enough to get the girls chattering and giggling. *Hormones.*

Sophie wasn't taking part in it, for once. She sat quietly for a moment, but I had no doubt she wasn't finished with her questions. Her mind was working a hundred miles an hour. When he parked in my driveway, she said, "Can we start now?"

MORE THAN HALF the team had come to the practice facility today, including a few of the guys who didn't have families.

Like 501.

He was here as a favor to me—there wasn't any point in trying to think he'd come for any other reason—but the fact was, he was here.

It was a Saturday afternoon in early March. With the playoffs only a little over a month away, the other coaches and I had decided the guys needed a break. A day with their families would do a lot more for how they played each night than another tedious practice going over the same systems and strategies we'd been pounding into their heads all season.

Soupy was still recovering from ACL surgery much earlier in the season, so he couldn't get out on the ice, but he and Rachel had brought all their kids. Rachel was busy suiting their twin toddlers up to go out on a sled that one of the young, single guys would pull around. Soupy had his bad leg propped up on a bench and was helping tie the skate laces for one of Dominic "Bear" Medved's kids. Tuck and Maddie Campbell were already out on the ice, as were Nicky Ericsson and his adopted niece and nephews, Marc "Danger" d'Aragon's teenagers, Grant "Wheels" Wheelan and his teens, and Mitch and Mia Quincey with their two little ones.

Babs and 501 were over on the other side of the ice, along with Webs and Drywall. All four of them were huddled up and bent over, no doubt putting finishing touches on Sophie's rig.

I'd carried in a bag of skates for Paige and the girls, and I dropped it on the bench next to Cam and Sara Johnson. Sara was bouncing their newborn in her arms while Jonny sat on the floor tying three-year-old Connor's skates. Connor, meanwhile, was bopping a Minion toy on his father's head. It kept saying unintelligible things with every hit, but then it said something that sounded distinctly like, "What the fuck?"

Connor giggled maniacally and repeated it. "What the fuck? What the fuck? What the fuck?"

"What did I tell you about not using Mommy's bad words?" Jonny said.

His son laughed even more fiendishly than before.

I did my best not to laugh out loud while I bent over to unload skates and other gear for my crew, but I saw Jonny calmly take the toy out of his son's hand, put it in their diaper bag, and give his wife a look that had her rolling her eyes.

"Don't blame that one on me," she said. "It's a toy."

When I handed Zoe the skates in her size, she was fighting the urge to bust up. I shook my head slightly, and she put a lid on it and took her skates.

Once Paige started helping the older girls get ready, I turned to Sophie.

She was bouncing on the balls of her feet and staring out at the ice. "Do I really get to skate, Bergy?"

"You really get to skate," I said. "So that means we need to put your gear on." I picked up her skates, kneepads, and helmet and took a seat. When she turned to look at me, grin a mile wide, I patted the spot on the bench next to me. She raced over and sat down.

By the time I had her properly outfitted, Babs and 501 were on their way around to join us with her rig.

Her older sisters giggled and made their nervous sounds, but not Sophie. She looked up and beamed at him. "Hi, Levi."

"Hi, Sophie. You ready to skate with me?"

She nodded emphatically and tried to stand up, but she wobbled on the skates.

I took her by the waist and steadied her, and the two brothers and I got her all strapped in. Drywall came over to be sure we had her situated right and all his measurements had been correct.

"Told you I could do this," he said, slapping me on the back after he'd completed his inspection.

"So I can skate?" Sophie squealed.

"You can skate," I said. I took one of her hands and 501 took the other, and we helped her walk cautiously to the door with her backward walker on skis coming behind her. When we got there, I picked her up and set her on the ice.

Then 501 took over. He took both her hands and skated backward, pulling her along with him. "You've gotta bend your knees," he said to her. "Get down low and push your skates into the ice."

In no time, they were too far away for me to hear them anymore. I could hear the other girls coming up behind me thanks to their giggles. Evie and Izzy stepped onto the ice and almost fell. They decided to take the easy path around the boards so they'd have something to hold on to.

Zoe stopped by my side before joining her sisters, though. "Hey, Bergy?"

I kept my eyes on 501 and Sophie to be sure that her rig was supporting her the way we intended it to. So far, so good. "Yeah?" I replied.

"I was just wanted to tell you that I've been talking to my sisters."

I chuckled. "No surprise there."

"Yeah. But we all agree."

Now I was curious. To my knowledge, they never agreed on anything but the fact that they needed to kidnap 501 and convince him to stay with them forever. "Agree about what?"

"Well, you know about the whole brother-husband thing?"

I nodded, internally cringing.

"Well, we think you should be Mom's brother-husband. Only there should just be you."

I definitely hadn't been expecting that one. "Don't you think that's moving a little—"

Before I could finish my question, she was rushing to catch up to the group of teens congregating on the opposite end of the ice.

I stayed in place for a few minutes, watching 501 and Sophie skate circles. She wasn't doing much of the work, letting him drag her along with him, but she lit up the entire rink with her smile. Even better, though, the rig was doing its job. It was supporting her weight while she found her legs and gained her balance. She might not ever get to the point that she could skate without it, but I wouldn't put it past her. Not when she was clearly having the time of her life. That would only make her want to work harder to make it happen.

Paige came up behind me and put her hand on my arm.

"She's doing great," I said.

Paige sniffled.

I spun around to face her and used my thumb to brush away the tears falling down her cheeks. "Hey," I said. "What's this about?"

"I didn't think this would ever happen," she said, shaking her head and waving her hand toward Sophie and 501. "She's doing things even I thought would be impossible, and it's all because of you."

"Not because of me."

She laughed through her tears. "Okay, fine. All because of Beefy, then."

I wrapped my arms around her and held her close, resting my chin on the top of her head. Not that I agreed with her assessment, but it wasn't worth arguing over. I was just glad to hold her for a while.

Over the last several weeks, I'd spent more and more time with Paige and her daughters whenever the team was in town. We weren't shy about showing physical affection for each other in front of them, but we kept it all on a PG level. The girls had started giving me hugs and acting like I was a normal fixture in their lives instead of an outsider they had to be on their best behavior for, and there had even been a few nights when, after the girls had gone to bed, Paige had snuck me up to her room before sending me on my way. I wasn't about to spend the night with the girls in the house. That seemed like stepping way over the line. But I couldn't deny that I liked the thought behind Zoe's suggestion even if it might be too soon to take that kind of step. It was something to think about.

Something to talk to Paige about, but preferably not when we were surrounded by half my team and their families.

She broke away from me and angled her head toward a quiet corner. I took her hand and followed her, trusting that 501 and Sophie's rig would be enough to take care of her, and that the other girls were fine with the rest of the teens.

When she came to a stop, she stretched up on her toes and kissed me.

I laughed out loud. "I didn't realize it was kissy-kissy time."

"I think it's always kissy-kissy time when I'm around you. I think about you all the time. About how you don't just care about me but you care about my girls, too. About how you take time out of your life to be with all of us. You're like a dream, Mattias, except you're real."

"You're my dream," I said, looking down into her rich, hazel eyes. She still had tears in them, but there was something else, too. Something deeper. It was as though I could see all the way to her heart just by looking in those eyes, and that heart was smiling back at me.

She bit down on her lip. "I just… I wasn't prepared

for this."

"Prepared for what?"

"For falling in love with you. But I have."

She could have blown me over with that, because I was in love with her, too. And her girls. And her life. The more time I spent in her house, surrounded by her family and the way they loved and supported each other, the more it felt like exactly where I needed to be. I'd thought it would take more to convince her we were meant to be together. I'd expected to have to work harder to find a way to fit within her life, and to convince her to let me in since she had to think about her daughters as well as herself.

But she loved me.

"That's good," I finally said, unable to wipe the goofy grin off my face.

"Why is that good?"

"Because I think I've been in love with you since not long after I met you. And I know I love your daughters."

"I know you love them. I think that's why I finally stopped fighting it. Because you're so good to them, and you're so devoted to Sophie. You work harder to make her life better than even her own father." Paige's tears started up again, so I drew her into my arms and held her to me. "He's a good man, but he just doesn't take the time to be there for her. But you do. All the time. I've spent so many years feeling like her sisters and I were the only ones fighting for her, and now it feels like a huge weight has been lifted."

If I wasn't careful, she was going to bring out some emotion in me that I'd kept locked away for a very long time. The last thing I needed was for my players to see me cry, so I put that under lock and key. It was one thing to laugh and smile in front of them; it was something else to let them see me being so vulnerable.

Once I thought I had it under control, I said, "I've got big shoulders, Paige. I can carry a lot."

"Mom!" Sophie screamed. My blood turned to ice, and we both spun around in panic.

But it was a good scream. A happy scream.

Because she was skating all by herself. Yes, she still had the rig holding her up. Yes, she was moving slowly and awkwardly, and if she didn't have the rig, she'd be on the ice in a heartbeat. But she was bending her knees and digging into the ice, and she was propelling herself forward, chasing 501, who was a few strides ahead of her.

"Oh," Paige said, and her hand shot up to cover her mouth as a fresh flood of tears streamed down her cheeks. "My baby's skating."

She wasn't the only one crying, either. As soon as I felt a hot tear blaze a trail down my own cheek, I brushed it away with the back of my hand. So maybe it wasn't the end of the world if my players saw me cry. Not if it was for the right reason, and this was definitely the right reason.

Epilogue

Paige

"Why isn't Bergy here yet?" Sophie asked. "He's late."

"He's not late," I replied, glancing at the clock on the wall. In the months he'd been in our lives, he had never once been late, and I doubted that would change today. He still had ten minutes before he was due to arrive.

"But he's not early, Mom," my youngest complained, and I laughed.

"Just because he's not early, that doesn't make him late," Evie pointed out.

"It does for Beefy," Izzy said.

I was inclined to side with Izzy on this one, not that I would say so in front of the girls. If Mattias said he would be somewhere at eight, you could count on him to show up at 7:45. It was just part of his makeup. So, like Sophie and Izzy, I wondered where he was and what had held him up.

Zoe tossed a throw pillow at her sister's head, her face bright red from the effort to stop a laugh combined with her continued embarrassment. "Stop calling him that."

The girls were on Spring Break, so I had taken the week off. It was the last week of the regular season, and the Storm were finishing things out at home, so Mattias was in Portland for now. He'd promised to pick us up after he got done with practice because he had a surprise for Sophie.

A surprise he hadn't even told me about, no less.

Before an argument broke out, the doorbell rang, and all four girls raced to open it.

"Bergy!" Sophie squealed as I rounded the corner and saw him for myself.

He had Sophie wrapped up with one arm and was holding another bouquet of yellow tulips with the other hand, and he winked at me over the top of them. "Sorry I'm late," he said. "I just remembered I hadn't brought your mom flowers since we got back in town."

The older girls giggled and took care of getting the tulips in water while Mattias and I gathered up purses and Sophie's backpack.

"You don't have to bring me flowers every time you come back from a trip, you know."

"I know," he said. "I like bringing you flowers, though."

"Why's that?"

"Because you light up with the prettiest smile when you see them. Almost as bright as Sophie's."

I laughed. "Well, that's saying something."

Within a few minutes, we were all in his SUV and he was backing out of my driveway.

"You still won't tell us where we're going, Bergy?"

Izzy asked.

"I guess I could tell you now." He gave me a look I couldn't interpret. "I'm taking you to an ice skating rink where a kids' hockey team practices."

"A hockey team?" Sophie repeated, her excitement creeping into her tone.

"Yeah. For kids your age, Sophie."

I caught his eye and shook my head. She'd been skating with her rig every day for weeks, as often as either Mattias or I could get her to the Storm's practice facility. And she was definitely making improvements, but that didn't mean she was ready for something more. She still needed the supportive structure to hold her up. Her core wasn't strong enough for her to balance on skate blades.

"I'm going to play hockey?" She was bouncing so hard in her seat that I could hear it.

"We're going to talk to the coach and find out if you can play next year," he said.

"But *you're* the coach, Bergy."

"Not for this team, I'm not. Coach Carlson is a special coach, and he works with extra special kids."

Special kids. Meaning kids with special needs. I caught the hidden meaning even if Sophie might not have, and I decided to reserve judgment until I could see what this program was all about for myself.

And once I saw what they were all about and heard the coach tell Sophie all the things she would have to do between now and next October if she was going to be able to play with the rest of the special needs kids? I nearly started crying.

Coach Carlson let Sophie put on all her gear, including strapping into her rig, and get out on the ice with the rest of his team. He gave her a hockey stick, and the rest of us watched from the stands as one of the other kids taught her how to shoot the puck toward the net.

"She's really going to play hockey, isn't she?" Zoe said, sniffling.

Mattias nodded. "Yeah. I think so."

I was too overwrought to do anything but take his hand and squeeze.

For the next half hour, we sat there and witnessed Sophie beginning to realize her dream. Once the kids started to leave the ice, Mattias climbed down the bleachers and helped the coach get Sophie out of her gear.

"Mom?" Zoe asked once he was well out of our hearing.

"Hmm?"

"I think he's a keeper."

I laughed, still sniffling. "Oh, you do, huh?"

"Yeah," Izzy said.

"Definitely," Evie added. "He's not the kind of guy you let get away from you. So you need to do something about that."

I got the distinct sense that my girls were ganging up on me, and I wasn't sure what to do about it. "Do something about it like what?"

Izzy shrugged, and Evie said, "I don't know."

But Zoe didn't brush it off. "Something like asking him to come live with us."

"What?" I didn't even attempt to hide my shock. That wasn't something we'd ever talked about, whether my girls were around or not. "Why do you think he should come live with us?"

"Because you love him. So do we." Zoe gave me a look that clearly said I was being slow. "It just makes sense."

"What makes sense?" Mattias asked when he and Sophie clomped back up the stairs.

"You coming to live with us," Izzy answered.

He nodded, looking at her before turning his gaze to each of my girls in turn. Then he settled that gaze on me, and I nearly melted into the aluminum bench I was sitting on. "Is everyone on board with that?" he asked cautiously.

"Yes!"

"Absolutely."

"Mm-hmm."

My daughters were going to be the death of me.

Sophie was still holding his hand, and she tugged on it until he looked down at her. "Will you come live with us?" she asked.

He squeezed her hand and winked before looking over at me. "I don't know. I guess it depends on what your mom has to say about that."

"Oh, please, Mom!" she said. "I need Bergy to help me skate. I got to get a lot better by next year so I can play hockey."

Her sisters chimed in with a chorus of "Please," not that it would have made a difference. I already knew what I wanted, and I already knew what I thought would be best for not only myself but also my daughters.

I narrowed my eyes up at him. "I say," I said slowly, "that if Beefy wants to come live with us, he can. But only if he keeps bringing me flowers every now and then. And maybe if we can arrange to meet his sister sometime this summer."

He laughed. "It's a deal."

And we all knew how Mattias felt about deals. Once

he made a deal with someone, he followed through on his end of it.

About the Author

Catherine Gayle is a *USA Today* bestselling author of Regency-set historical romance and contemporary hockey romance. She's a transplanted Texan living in North Carolina with two extremely spoiled felines. In her spare time, she watches way too much hockey and reality TV, plans fun things to do for the Nephew Monster's next visit, and performs experiments in the kitchen which are rarely toxic.

Visit her website at www.catherinegayle.com. Join her mailing list at http://eepurl.com/GXcwr to receive news about new releases, sales, and pre-orders, as well as to receive a free Portland Storm short story titled ICE BREAKER, which is not available for sale through any outlet.

Other Books by Catherine Gayle

Breakaway
On the Fly
Taking a Shot
Light the Lamp
Delay of Game
Double Major
In the Zone
Holiday Hat Trick
Comeback
Dropping Gloves
Bury the Hatchet
Home Ice
Smoke Signals
Mistletoe Misconduct
Losing an Edge
Ghost Dance

Dreaming Up a Dare
Game Breaker
Twice a Rake
Saving Grace
Merely a Miss
Wallflower
Pariah
Seven Minutes in Devon
Flight of Fancy
Rhyme and Reason
Thick as Thieves
An Unintended Journey
To Enchant an Icy Earl
The Devil to Pay
A Dance with the Devil
Wanton Wives